PENGUIN BOOKS

THE MAN WITH THE GOLDEN GUN

Ian Fleming was born in 1908 and educated at Eton. After a brief period at the Royal Military Academy at Sandhurst he went abroad to further his education. In 1931, having failed to get an appointment in the Foreign Office, he joined Reuters News Agency. During the Second World War he was Personal Assistant to the Director of Naval Intelligence at the Admiralty, rising to the rank of Commander. His wartime experiences provided him with a first-hand knowledge of secret operations.

After the war he became Foreign Manager of Kemsley Newspapers. He built his house, Goldeneye, in Jamaica and there at the age of forty-four he wrote *Casino Royale*, the first of the novels featuring Commander James Bond. By the time of his death in 1964, the James Bond adventures had sold more than forty million copies. *Doctor No*, the first film featuring James Bond and starring Sean Connery, was released in 1962 and the Bond films continue to be huge international successes. He is also the author of the magical children's book *Chitty Chitty Bang Bang*.

The novels of Ian Fleming were immediately recognized as classic thrillers by his contemporaries Kingsley Amis, Raymond Chandler and John Betjeman. With the invention of James Bond, Ian Fleming created the greatest British fictional icon of the late twentieth century.

For more information about Ian Fleming's life and works, please visit the official Web site of Ian Fleming Publications Ltd: www.ianflemingcentre.com.

THE JAMES BOND BOOKS

Casino Royale

Live and Let Die

Moonraker

Diamonds are Forever

From Russia with Love

Doctor No

Goldfinger

For Your Eyes Only

Thunderball

The Spy Who Loved Me

On Her Majesty's Secret Service

You Only Live Twice

The Man with the Golden Gun

Octopussy/The Living Daylights

the Man with the Golden Gun

A JAMES BOND NOVEL

007

BY IAN FLEMING

PENGUIN BOOKS

PENGUIN BOOKS

Published by the Penguin Group

Penguin Group (USA) Inc., 375 Hudson Street, New York, New York 10014, U.S.A.

Penguin Group (Canada), 90 Eglinton Avenue East, Suite 700, Toronto,
    Ontario, Canada M4P 2Y3 (a division of Pearson Penguin Canada Inc.)

Penguin Books Ltd, 80 Strand, London WC2R 0RL, England

Penguin Ireland, 25 St Stephen's Green, Dublin 2, Ireland (a division of Penguin Books Ltd)

Penguin Group (Australia), 250 Camberwell Road, Camberwell,
    Victoria 3124, Australia (a division of Pearson Australia Group Pty Ltd)

Penguin Books India Pvt Ltd, 11 Community Centre, Panchsheel Park, New Delhi – 110 017, India

Penguin Group (NZ), cnr Airborne and Rosedale Roads,
    Albany, Auckland 1310, New Zealand (a division of Pearson New Zealand Ltd)

Penguin Books (South Africa) (Pty) Ltd, 24 Sturdee Avenue,
    Rosebank, Johannesburg 2196, South Africa

Penguin Books Ltd, Registered Offices: 80 Strand, London WC2R 0RL, England

First published in Great Britain by Jonathan Cape Ltd. 1965
First published in the United States by New American Library 1966
Published in Penguin Books (U.K.) 2002
Published in Penguin Books (U.S.A.) 2004

10 9 8 7

ISBN 0 14 20.0328 X
CIP data available

Printed in the United States of America
Set in Melior

CONTENTS

The Secret Service holds much that is kept secret even from very senior officers in the organization. Only M and his Chief of Staff know absolutely everything there is to know. The latter is responsible for keeping the Top Secret record known as 'The War Book' so that, in the event of the death of both of them, the whole story, apart from what is available to individual Sections and Stations, would be available to their successors.

One thing that James Bond, for instance, didn't know was the machinery at Headquarters for dealing with the public, whether friendly or otherwise—drunks, lunatics, bona fide applications to join the Service, and enemy agents with plans for penetration or even assassination.

On that cold, clear morning in November he was to see the careful cog-wheels in motion.

The girl at the switchboard at the Ministry of Defence flicked the switch to 'Hold' and said to her neighbour, 'It's another nut who says he's James Bond. Even knows his code number. Says he wants to speak to M personally.'

The senior girl shrugged. The switchboard had had quite a

few such calls since, a year before, James Bond's death on a mission to Japan had been announced in the Press. There had even been one pestiferous woman who, at every full moon, passed on messages from Bond from Uranus where it seemed he had got stuck while awaiting entry into heaven. She said, 'Put him through to Liaison, Pat.'

The Liaison Section was the first cog in the machine, the first sieve. The operator got back on the line: 'Just a moment, sir. I'll put you on to an officer who may be able to help you.'

James Bond, sitting on the edge of his bed, said, 'Thank you.'

He had expected some delay before he could establish his identity. He had been warned to expect it by the charming 'Colonel Boris' who had been in charge of him for the past few months after he had finished his treatment in the luxurious Institute on the Nevsky Prospekt in Leningrad. A man's voice came on the line. 'Captain Walker speaking. Can I help you?'

James Bond spoke slowly and clearly. 'This is Commander James Bond speaking. Number 007. Would you put me through to M, or his secretary, Miss Moneypenny. I want to make an appointment.'

Captain Walker pressed two buttons on the side of his telephone. One of them switched on a tape recorder for the use of his department, the other alerted one of the duty officers in the Action Room of the Special Branch at Scotland Yard that he should listen to the conversation, trace the call, and at once put a tail on the caller. It was now up to Captain Walker, who was in fact an extremely bright ex-prisoner-of-war interrogator from Military Intelligence, to keep the subject talking for as near five minutes as possible. He said, 'I'm afraid I don't know either of these two people. Are you sure you've got the right number?'

James Bond patiently repeated the Regent number which was the main outside line for the Secret Service. Together with so much else, he had forgotten it, but Colonel Boris had known it and had made him write it down among the small print on the front page of his forged British passport that said his name was Frank Westmacott, company director.

'Yes,' said Captain Walker sympathetically. 'We seem to have got that part of it right. But I'm afraid I can't place these people you want to talk to. Who exactly are they? This Mr Em, for instance. I don't think we've got anyone of that name at the Ministry.'

'Do you want me to spell it out? You realize this is an open line?'

Captain Walker was rather impressed by the confidence in the speaker's voice. He pressed another button and, so that Bond would hear it, a telephone bell rang. He said, 'Hang on a moment, would you? There's someone on my other line.' Captain Walker got on to the head of his Section. 'Sorry, sir. I've got a chap on who says he's James Bond and wants to talk to M. I know it sounds crazy and I've gone through the usual motions with the Special Branch and so on, but would you mind listening for a minute? Thank you, sir.'

Two rooms away a harassed man, who was the Chief Security Officer for the Secret Service, said 'Blast!' and pressed a switch. A microphone on his desk came to life. The Chief Security Officer sat very still. He badly needed a cigarette, but his room was now 'live' to Captain Walker and to the lunatic who called himself 'James Bond'. Captain Walker's voice came over at full strength. 'I'm sorry. Now then. This man Mr Em you want to talk to. I'm sure we needn't worry about security. Could you be more specific?'

James Bond frowned. He didn't know that he had frowned and he wouldn't have been able to explain why he had done so. He said, and lowered his voice, again inexplicably, 'Admiral Sir Miles Messervy. He is head of a department in your Ministry. The number of his room used to be twelve on the eighth floor. He used to have a secretary called Miss Moneypenny. Good-looking girl. Brunette. Shall I give you the Chief of Staff's name? No? Well let's see, it's Wednesday. Shall I tell you what'll be the main dish on the menu in the canteen? It should be steak-and-kidney pudding.'

The Chief Security Officer picked up the direct telephone to Captain Walker. Captain Walker said to James Bond, 'Damn! There's the other telephone again. Shan't be a minute.' He picked up the green telephone. 'Yes, sir?'

'I don't like that bit about the steak-and-kidney pudding. Pass him on to the Hard Man. No. Cancel that. Make it the Soft. There was always something odd about 007's death. No body. No solid evidence. And the people on that Japanese island always seemed to me to be playing it pretty close to the chest. The Stone Face act. It's just possible. Keep me informed, would you?'

Captain Walker got back to James Bond. 'Sorry about that. It's being a busy day. Now then, this inquiry of yours. Afraid I can't help you myself. Not my part of the Ministry. The man you want is Major Townsend. He should be able to locate this man you want to see. Got a pencil? It's No. 44 Kensington Cloisters. Got that? Kensington double five double five. Give me ten minutes and I'll have a word with him and see if he can help. All right?'

James Bond said dully, 'That's very kind of you.' He put down the telephone. He waited exactly ten minutes and picked up the receiver and asked for the number.

James Bond was staying at the Ritz Hotel. Colonel Boris had told him to do so. Bond's file in the KGB Archive described him as a high-liver, so, on arrival in London, he must stick to the KGB image of the high life. Bond went down in the lift to the Arlington Street entrance. A man at the newsstand got a good profile of him with a buttonhole Minox. When Bond went down the shallow steps to the street and asked the commissionaire for a taxi, a canonflex with a telescopic lens clicked away busily from a Red Roses laundry van at the neighbouring goods entrance and, in due course, the same van followed Bond's taxi while a man inside the van reported briefly to the Action Room of the Special Branch.

No. 44 Kensington Cloisters was a dull Victorian mansion in grimy red brick. It had been chosen for its purpose because it had once been the headquarters of the Empire League for Noise Abatement, and its entrance still bore the brass plate of this long-defunct organization, the empty shell of which had been purchased by the Secret Service through the Commonwealth Relations Office. It also had a spacious old-fashioned basement, re-equipped as detention cells, and a rear exit into a quiet mews.

The Red Roses laundry van watched the front door shut behind James Bond and then moved off at a sedate speed to its garage not far from Scotland Yard while the process of developing the canonflex film went on in its interior.

'Appointment with Major Townsend,' said Bond.

'Yes. He's expecting you, sir. Shall I take your raincoat?' The powerful-looking doorman put the coat on a coat-hanger and hung it up on one of a row of hooks beside the door. As soon as Bond was safely closeted with Major Townsend, the coat would go swiftly to the laboratory on the first floor where its provenance would be established from an examination of the fabric. Pocket dust would be removed for more leisurely research. 'Would you follow me, sir?'

It was a narrow corridor of freshly painted clapboard with a tall, single window which concealed the Fluoroscope triggered automatically from beneath the ugly patterned carpet. The findings of its X-ray eye would be fed into the laboratory above the passage. The passage ended in two facing doors marked 'A' and 'B'. The doorman knocked on Room B and stood aside for Bond to enter.

It was a pleasant, very light room, close-carpeted in dove-grey Wilton. The military prints on the cream walls were expensively framed. A small, bright fire burned under an Adam mantelpiece which bore a number of silver trophies and two photographs in leather frames—one of a nice-looking woman and the other of three nice-looking children. There was a central table with a bowl of flowers and two comfortable club chairs on either side of the fire. No desk or filing cabinets, nothing official-looking. A tall man, as pleasant as the room, got up from the far chair, dropped *The Times* on the carpet beside it, and came forward with a welcoming smile. He held out a firm, dry hand.

This was the Soft Man.

'Come in. Come in. Take a pew. Cigarette? Not the ones I seem to remember you favour. Just the good old Senior Service.'

Major Townsend had carefully prepared the loaded remark—a reference to Bond's liking for the Morland Specials with the three gold rings. He noted Bond's apparent lack of comprehension. Bond took a cigarette and accepted a light. They sat down facing one another. Major Townsend crossed his legs comfortably. Bond sat up straight. Major Townsend said, 'Well now. How can I help you?'

Across the corridor, in Room A, a cold Office-of-Works cube with no furniture but a hissing gas fire, an ugly desk with two facing wooden chairs under the naked neon, Bond's reception by the Hard Man, the ex-police superintendent ('ex' because of a brutality case in Glasgow for which he had taken the rap) would have been very different. There, the man who went under the name of Mr Robson would have given him the full intimidation treatment— harsh, bullying interrogation, threats of imprisonment for false representation and God knows what else, and, perhaps, if he had shown signs of hostility or developing a nuisance value, a little judicious roughing-up in the basement.

Such was the ultimate sieve which sorted out the wheat from the chaff from those members of the public who desired access to 'The Secret Service'. There were other people in the building who dealt with the letters. Those written in pencil or in multi-coloured inks, and those enclosing a photograph, remained unanswered. Those which threatened or were litigious were referred to the Special Branch. The solid, serious ones were passed, with a comment from the best graphologist in the business, to the Liaison Section at Headquarters for 'further action'. Parcels went automatically, and fast, to the Bomb Disposal Squad at Knightsbridge Barracks. The eye of the needle was narrow. On the whole, it discriminated appropriately. It was an expensive set-up, but it is the first duty of a Secret Service to remain not only secret but secure.

There was no reason why James Bond, who had always been on the operative side of the business, should know anything about the entrails of the service, any more than he should have understood the mysteries of the plumbing or electricity supply of his flat in Chelsea, or the working of his own kidneys. Colonel Boris, however, had known the whole routine. The secret services of all the great powers know the public face of their opponents, and Colonel Boris had very accurately described the treatment that James Bond must expect before he was 'cleared' and was allowed access to the office of his former chief.

So now James Bond paused before he replied to Major Townsend's question about how he could be of help. He looked at the Soft Man and then into the fire. He added up the accuracy of the description he had been given of Major Townsend's appearance and, before he said what he had been told to say, he gave Colonel Boris ninety out of a hundred. The big, friendly face, the wide-apart, pale-brown eyes, bracketed by the wrinkles of a million smiles, the military moustache, the rimless monocle dangling from a thin black cord, the brushed-back, thinning sandy hair, the immaculate double-breasted blue suit, stiff white collar and Brigade tie— it was all there. But what Colonel Boris hadn't said was that the friendly eyes were as cold and steady as gun barrels and that the lips were thin and scholarly.

James Bond said patiently: 'It's really quite simple. I'm who I say I am. I'm doing what I naturally would do, and that's report back to M.'

'Quite. But you must realize' (a sympathetic smile) 'that you've been out of contact for nearly a year. You've been officially posted as "missing believed killed". Your obituary has even appeared in *The Times*. Have you any evidence of identity? I admit that you look very much like your photographs, but you must see that we have to be very sure before we pass you on up the ladder.'

'A Miss Mary Goodnight was my secretary. She'd recognize me all right. So would dozens of other people at HQ.'

'Miss Goodnight's been posted abroad. Can you give me a brief description of HQ, just the main geography?'

Bond did so.

'Right. Now, who was a Miss Maria Freudenstadt?'

'Was?'

'Yes, she's dead.'

'Thought she wouldn't last long. She was a double, working for KGB. Section 100 controlled her. I wouldn't get any thanks for telling you any more.'

Major Townsend had been primed with this very secret top question. He had been given the answer, more or less as Bond had put it. This was the clincher. This *had* to be James Bond. 'Well, we're getting on fine. Now, it only remains to find out where you've come from and where you've been all these months and I won't keep you any longer.'

'Sorry. I can only tell that to M personally.'

'I see.' Major Townsend put on a thoughtful expression. 'Well, just let me make a telephone call or two and I'll see what can be done.' He got to his feet. 'Seen today's *Times*?' He picked it up and handed it to Bond. It had been specially treated to give good prints. Bond took it. 'Shan't be long.'

Major Townsend shut the door behind him and went across the passage and through the door marked 'A' where he knew that 'Mr Robson' would be alone. 'Sorry to bother you, Fred. Can I use your scrambler?' The chunky man behind the desk grunted through the stem of his pipe and remained bent over the midday *Evening Standard* racing news.

Major Townsend picked up the green receiver and was put through to the Laboratory. 'Major Townsend speaking. Any comment?' He listened, carefully, said 'thank you', and got through to the Chief Security Officer at Headquarters. 'Well, sir, I think it must be 007. Bit thinner than his photographs. I'll be giving you his prints as soon as he's gone. Wearing his usual rig—dark-blue single-breasted suit, white shirt, thin black knitted silk tie, black casuals—but they all look brand new. Raincoat bought yesterday from Burberry's. Got the Freudenstadt question right, but says he won't say anything about himself except to M personally. But whoever he is, I don't like it much. He fluffed on his special cigarettes. He's got an odd sort of glazed, sort of far-away look, and the "Scope" shows that he's carrying a gun in his right-hand coat pocket—curious sort of contraption, doesn't seem to have got a butt to it. I'd say he's a sick man. I wouldn't personally recommend that M should see him, but I wouldn't know how we're to get him to talk unless he does.' He paused. 'Very good, sir. I'll stay by the telephone. I'm on Mr Robson's extension.'

There was silence in the room. The two men didn't get on well together. Major Townsend gazed into the gas fire, wondering about the man next door. The telephone burred. 'Yes, sir? Very good, sir. Would your secretary send along a car from the pool? Thank you, sir.'

Bond was sitting in the same upright posture, *The Times* still unopened in his hand. Major Townsend said cheerfully, 'Well, that's fixed. Message from M that he's tremendously relieved you're all right and he'll be free in about half an hour. Car should be here in ten minutes or so. And the Chief of Staff says he hopes you'll be free for lunch afterwards.'

James Bond smiled for the first time. It was a thin smile which didn't light up his eyes. He said, 'That's very kind of him. Would you tell him I'm afraid I shan't be free.'

The Chief of Staff stood in front of M's desk and said firmly, 'I really wouldn't do it, sir. I can see him, or someone else can. I don't like the smell of it at all. I think 007's round the bend. There's no doubt it's him all right. The prints have just been confirmed by Chief of Security. And the pictures are all right—and the recording of his voice. But there are too many things that don't add up. This forged passport we found in his room at the Ritz, for instance. All right. So he wanted to come back into the country quietly. But it's too good a job. Typical KGB sample. And the last entry is West Germany, day before yesterday. Why didn't he report to Station B or W? Both those Heads of Station are friends of his, particularly 016 in Berlin. And why didn't he go and have a look at his flat? He's got some sort of a housekeeper there, Scots woman called May, who's always sworn he was still alive and has kept the place going on her savings. The Ritz is sort of "stage" Bond. And these new clothes. Why did he have to bother? Doesn't matter what he was wearing when he came in through Dover. Normal thing, if he was in rags, would have been to give me a ring—he had my home number—and get me to fix him up. Have a few drinks and run over his story and then report here. Instead of that we've got this typical penetration approach and Security worried as hell.'

The Chief of Staff paused. He knew he wasn't getting through. As soon as he had begun, M had swivelled his chair sideways and had remained, occasionally sucking at an unlighted pipe, gazing moodily out through the window at the jagged sky-line of London. Obstinately, the Chief of Staff concluded, 'Do you think you could leave this one to me, sir? I can get hold of Sir James Molony in no time and have 007 put into The Park for observation and treatment. It'll all be done very gently. VIP handling and so on. I can say you've been called to the Cabinet or something. Security says 007's looking a bit thin. Build him up. Convalescence and all that. That can be the excuse. If he cuts up rough, we can always give him some dope. He's a good friend of mine. He won't hold it against us. He obviously needs to be got back in the groove—if we can do it, that is.'

M slowly swivelled his chair round. He looked up at the tired, worried face that showed the strain of being the equivalent of Number Two in the Secret Service for ten years and more. M smiled. 'Thank you, Chief of Staff. But I'm afraid it's not as easy as all that. I sent 007 out on his last job to shake him out of his domestic worries. You remember how it all came about. Well, we had no idea that what seemed a fairly peaceful mission was going to end up in a pitched battle with Blofeld. Or that 007 was going to vanish off the face of the earth for a year. Now we've got to know what happened during that year. And 007's quite right. I sent him out on that mission and he's got every right to report back to me personally. I know 007. He's a stubborn fellow. If he says he won't tell anyone else, he won't. Of course I want to hear what happened to him. You'll listen in. Have a couple of good men at hand. If he turns rough, come and get him. As for his gun'— M gestured vaguely at the ceiling—'I can look after that. Have you tested the damned thing?'

'Yes, sir. It works all right. But . . .'

M held up a hand. 'Sorry, Chief of Staff. It's an order.' A light winked on the intercom. 'That'll be him. Send him straight in, would you?'

'Very good, sir.' The Chief of Staff went out and closed the door.

James Bond was standing smiling vaguely down at Miss Moneypenny. She looked distraught. When James Bond shifted his gaze and said 'Hullo, Bill' he still wore the same distant smile. He didn't hold out his hand. Bill Tanner said, with a heartiness that rang with a terrible falsity in his ears, 'Hullo, James. Long time no see.' At the same time, out of the corner of his eye, he saw Miss Moneypenny give a quick, emphatic shake of the head. He looked her straight in the eyes. 'M would like to see 007 straight away.'

Miss Moneypenny lied desperately: 'You know M's got a Chiefs of Staff meeting at the Cabinet Office in five minutes?'

'Yes. He says you must somehow get him out of it.' The Chief of Staff turned to James Bond. 'Okay, James. Go ahead. Sorry you can't manage lunch. Come and have a gossip after M's finished with you.'

Bond said, 'That'll be fine.' He squared his shoulders and walked through the door over which the red light was already burning.

Miss Moneypenny buried her face in her hands. 'Oh, Bill!' she said desperately. 'There's something wrong with him. I'm frightened.'

Bill Tanner said, 'Take it easy, Penny. I'm going to do what

I can.' He walked quickly into his office and shut the door. He went over to his desk and pressed a switch. M's voice came into the room: 'Hullo, James. Wonderful to have you back. Take a seat and tell me all about it.'

Bill Tanner picked up the office telephone and asked for Head of Security.

James Bond took his usual place across the desk from M. A storm of memories whirled through his consciousness like badly cut film on a projector that had gone crazy. Bond closed his mind to the storm. He must concentrate on what he had to say, and do, and on nothing else.

'I'm afraid there's a lot I still can't remember, sir. I got a bang on the head' (he touched his right temple) 'somewhere along the line on that job you sent me to do in Japan. Then there's a blank until I got picked up by the police on the waterfront at Vladivostok. No idea how I got there. They roughed me up a bit and in the process I must have got another bang on the head because suddenly I remembered who I was and that I wasn't a Japanese fisherman which was what I thought I was. So then of course the police passed me on to the local branch of the KGB—it's a big grey building on the Morskaya Ulitsa facing the harbour near the railway station, by the way—and when they belinographed my prints to Moscow there was a lot of excitement and they flew me there from the military airfield just north of the town at Vtoraya Rechka and spent weeks interrogating me—or trying to, rather, because I couldn't remember anything except when they prompted me with something they knew themselves and then I could give them a few hazy details to add to their knowledge. Very frustrating for them.'

'Very,' commented M. A small frown had gathered between his eyes. 'And you told them everything you could? Wasn't that rather, er, generous of you?'

'They were very nice to me in every way, sir. It seemed the least I could do. There was this Institute place in Leningrad. They gave me VIP treatment. Top brain-specialists and everything. They didn't seem to hold it against me that I'd been working against them for most of my life. And other people came and talked to me very reasonably about the political situation and so forth. The need for East and West to work together for world peace. They made clear a lot of things that hadn't occurred to me before. They quite convinced me.' Bond looked obstinately across the table into the clear blue sailor's eyes that now held a red spark of anger. 'I don't suppose you understand what I mean, sir. You've been making war against someone or other all your life. You're doing so at this moment. And for most of my adult life you've used me as a tool. Fortunately that's all over now.'

M said fiercely, 'It certainly is. I suppose among other things you've forgotten is reading reports of our POWs in the Korean war who were brainwashed by the Chinese. If the Russians are so keen on peace, what do they need the KGB for? At the last estimate, that was about one hundred thousand men and women "making war" as you call it against us and other countries. This is the organization that was so charming to you in Leningrad. Did they happen to mention the murder of Horcher and Stutz in Munich last month?'

'Oh yes, sir.' Bond's voice was patient, equable. 'They have to defend themselves against the secret services of the West. If you would demobilize all this,' Bond waved a hand, 'they would be only too delighted to scrap the KGB. They were quite open about it all.'

'And the same thing applies to their two hundred divisions and their U-boat fleet and their ICBMs, I suppose?' M's voice rasped.

'Of course, sir.'

'Well, if you found these people so reasonable and charming, why didn't you stay there? Others have. Burgess is dead, but you could have chummed up with Maclean.'

'We thought it more important that I should come back and fight for peace here, sir. You and your agents have taught me certain skills for use in the underground war. It was explained to me how these skills could be used in the cause of peace.'

James Bond's hand moved nonchalantly to his right-hand coat pocket. M, with equal casualness, shifted his chair back from his desk. His left hand felt for the button under the arm of the chair.

'For instance?' said M quietly, knowing that death had walked into the room and was standing beside him and that this was an invitation for death to take his place in the chair.

James Bond had become tense. There was a whiteness round his lips. The blue-grey eyes still stared blankly, almost unseeingly at M. The words rang out harshly, as if forced out of him by some inner compulsion. 'It would be a start if the warmongers could be eliminated, sir. This is for number one on the list.'

The hand, snub-nosed with black metal, flashed out of the pocket, but, even as the poison hissed down the barrel of the bulb-butted pistol, the great sheet of Armourplate glass hurtled down from the baffled slit in the ceiling and, with a last sigh of hydraulics, braked to the floor. The jet of viscous brown fluid splashed harmlessly into its centre and trickled slowly down, distorting M's face and the arm he had automatically thrown up for additional protection.

The Chief of Staff had burst into the room, followed by the Head of Security. They threw themselves on James Bond. Even as they seized his arms his head fell forward on his chest and he would have slid from his chair to the ground if they hadn't supported him. They hauled him to his feet. He was in a dead faint. The Head of Security sniffed. 'Cyanide,' he said curtly. 'We must all get out of here. And bloody quick!' (The emergency had snuffed out Headquarters 'manners'.) The pistol lay on the carpet where it had fallen. He kicked it away. He said to M, who had walked out from behind his glass shield, 'Would you mind leaving the room, sir? Quickly. I'll have this cleaned up during the lunch hour.' It was an order. M went to the open door. Miss Moneypenny stood with her clenched hand up to her mouth. She watched with horror as James Bond's supine body was hauled out and, the heels of its shoes leaving tracks on the carpet, taken into the Chief of Staff's room.

M said sharply, 'Close that door, Miss Moneypenny. Get the duty MO up right away. Come along, girl! Don't just stand there gawking! And not a word of this to anyone. Understood?'

Miss Moneypenny pulled herself back from the edge of hysterics. She said an automatic 'Yes, sir', pulled the door shut and reached for the inter-office telephone.

M walked across and into the Chief of Staff's office and closed the door. Head of Security was on his knees beside Bond. He had loosened his tie and collar button and was feeling his pulse. Bond's face was white and bathed in sweat. His breathing was a desperate rattle, as if he had just run a race. M looked briefly down at him and then, his face hidden from the others, at the wall beyond the body. He turned to the Chief of Staff. He said briskly, 'Well, that's that. My predecessor died in that chair. Then it was a simple bullet, but from much the same sort of a crazed officer. One can't legislate against the lunatic. But the Office of Works certainly did a good job with that gadget. Now then, Chief of Staff. This is of course to go no further. Get Sir James Molony as soon as you can and have 007 taken down to The Park. Ambulance, surreptitious guard. I'll explain things to Sir James this afternoon. Briefly, as you heard, the KGB got hold of him. Brainwashed him. He was already a sick man. Amnesia of some kind. I'll tell you all I know later. Have his things collected from the Ritz and his bill paid. And put something out to the Press Association. Something on these lines: "The Ministry of Defence is pleased," no, say delighted, "to announce that Commander James Bond etc., who was posted as missing, believed killed while on a mission to Japan last November, has returned to this country after a hazardous journey across the Soviet Union which is expected to yield much valuable information. Commander Bond's health has inevitably suffered from his experiences and he is convalescing under medical supervision."' M smiled frostily. 'That bit about information'll give no joy to Comrade Semichastny and his troops. And add a "D" Notice to editors: "It is particularly requested, for security reasons, that the minimum of speculation or comment be added to the above communiqué and that no attempts be made to trace Commander Bond's whereabouts." All right?'

Bill Tanner had been writing furiously to keep up with M. He looked up from his scratch pad, bewildered. 'But aren't you going to make any charges, sir? After all, treason and attempted murder . . . I mean, not a court martial?'

'Certainly not.' M's voice was gruff. '007 was a sick man. Not responsible for his actions. If one can brainwash a man, presumably one can un-brainwash him. If anyone can, Sir James can. Put him back on half pay for the time being, in his old Section. And see he gets full back pay and allowances for the past year. If the KGB has the nerve to throw one of my best men at me, I have the nerve to throw him back at them. 007 was a good agent once. There's no reason why he shouldn't be a good agent again. Within limits, that is. After lunch, give me the file on Scaramanga. If we can get him fit again, that's the right-sized target for 007.'

The Chief of Staff protested, 'But that's suicide, sir! Even 007 could never take him.'

M said coldly, 'What would 007 get for this morning's bit of work? Twenty years? As a minimum, I'd say. Better for him to fall on the battlefield. If he brings it off, he'll have won his spurs back again and we can all forget the past. Anyway, that's my decision.'

There was a knock on the door and the duty Medical Officer came into the room. M bade him good afternoon and turned stiffly on his heel and walked out through the open door.

The Chief of Staff looked at the retreating back. He said, under his breath, 'You cold-hearted bastard!' Then, with his usual minute thoroughness and sense of duty, he set about the tasks he had been given. His not to reason why!

At Blades, M ate his usual meagre luncheon—a grilled Dover sole followed by the ripest spoonful he could gouge from the club Stilton. And as usual he sat by himself in one of the window seats and barricaded himself behind *The Times*, occasionally turning a page to demonstrate that he was reading it, which, in fact, he wasn't. But Porterfield commented to the head waitress, Lily, a handsome, much-loved ornament of the club, that 'there's something wrong with the old man today. Or maybe not exactly wrong, but there's something up with him.' Porterfield prided himself on being something of an amateur psychologist. As head waiter, and father confessor to many of the members, he knew a lot about all of them and liked to think he knew everything, so that, in the tradition of incomparable servants, he could anticipate their wishes and their moods. Now, standing with Lily in a quiet moment behind the finest cold buffet on display at that date anywhere in the world, he explained himself. 'You know that terrible stuff Sir Miles always drinks? That Algerian red wine that the wine committee won't even allow on the wine list. They only have it in the club to please Sir Miles. Well,

he explained to me once that in the navy they used to call it
"The Infuriator" because if you drank too much of it, it
seems that it used to put you into a rage. Well now, in the ten
years that I've had the pleasure of looking after Sir Miles,
he's never ordered more than half a carafe of the stuff.'
Porterfield's benign, almost priestly countenance assumed
an expression of theatrical solemnity as if he had read something really terrible in the tea leaves. 'Then what happens
today?' Lily clasped her hands tensely and bent her head
fractionally closer to get the full impact of the news. 'The old
man says, "Porterfield. A bottle of Infuriator. You understand? A full bottle!" So of course I didn't say anything but
went off and brought it to him. But mark my words, Lily,' he
noticed a lifted hand down the long room and moved off,
'there's something hit Sir Miles hard this morning and no
mistake.'

M sent for his bill. As usual he paid, whatever the amount
of the bill, with a five-pound note for the pleasure of receiving in change crisp new pound notes, new silver and gleaming copper pennies, for it is the custom at Blades to give its
members only freshly minted money. Porterfield pulled back
his table and M walked quickly to the door, acknowledging
the occasional greeting with a preoccupied nod and a brief
lifting of the hand. It was two o'clock. The old black Phan-
tom Rolls took him quietly and quickly northwards through
Berkeley Square, across Oxford Street and via Wigmore
Street into Regent's Park. M didn't look out at the passing
scene. He sat stiffly in the back, his bowler hat squarely set
on the middle of his head, and gazed unseeing at the back of
the chauffeur's head with hooded, brooding eyes.

For the hundredth time, since he had left his office that
morning, he assured himself that his decision was right. If

James Bond could be straightened out, and M was certain
that that supreme neurologist, Sir James Molony, could bring
it off, it would be ridiculous to re-assign him to normal staff
duties in the Double-O Section. The past could be forgiven,
but not forgotten—except with the passage of time. It would
be most irksome for those in the know to have Bond moving
about Headquarters as if nothing had happened. It would be
doubly embarrassing for M to have to face Bond across that
desk. And James Bond, if aimed straight at a known target—
M put it in the language of battleships—was a supremely
effective firing-piece. Well, the target was there and it desperately demanded destruction. Bond had accused M of
using him as a tool. Naturally. Every officer in the Service
was a tool for one secret purpose or another. The problem on
hand could only be solved by a killing. James Bond would
not possess the Double-O prefix if he had not high talents,
frequently proved, as a gunman. So be it! In exchange for the
happenings of that morning, in expiation of them, Bond
must prove himself at his old skills. If he succeeded, he
would have regained his previous status. If he failed, well, it
would be a death for which he would be honoured. Win or
lose, the plan would solve a vast array of problems. M closed
his mind once and for all on his decision. He got out of the
car and went up in the lift to the eighth floor and along the
corridor, smelling the smell of some unknown disinfectant
more and more powerfully as he approached his office.

Instead of using his key to the private entrance at the end
of the corridor M turned right through Miss Moneypenny's
door. She was sitting in her usual place, typing away at the
usual routine correspondence. She got to her feet.

'What's this dreadful stink, Miss Moneypenny?'

'I don't know what it's called, sir. Head of Security brought along a squad from Chemical Warfare at the War Office. He says your office is all right to use again but to keep the windows open for a while. So I've turned on the heating. Chief of Staff isn't back from lunch yet, but he told me to tell you that everything you wanted done is under way. Sir James is operating until four but will expect your call after that. Here's the file you wanted, sir.'

M took the brown folder with the red Top Secret star in its top right-hand corner. 'How's 007? Did he come round all right?'

Miss Moneypenny's face was expressionless. 'I gather so, sir. The MO gave him a sedative of some kind and he was taken off on a stretcher during the lunch hour. He was covered up. They took him down in the service lift to the garage. I haven't had any inquiries.'

'Good. Well, bring me in the signals, would you. There's been a lot of time wasted today on all these domestic excitements.' Bearing the file M went through the door into his office. Miss Moneypenny brought in the signals and stood dutifully beside him while he went through them, occasionally dictating a comment or a query. She looked down at the bowed, iron-grey head with the bald patch polished for years by a succession of naval caps and wondered, as she had wondered so often over the past ten years, whether she loved or hated this man. One thing was certain. She respected him more than any man she had known or had read of.

M handed her the file. 'Thank you. Now just give me a quarter of an hour, and then I'll see whoever wants me. The call to Sir James has priority of course.'

M opened the brown folder, reached for his pipe and began absent-mindedly filling it as he glanced through the list of subsidiary files to see if there was any other docket he

immediately needed. Then he set a match to his pipe and
settled back in his chair and read:

'FRANCISCO (PACO) "PISTOLS" SCARAMANGA.' And
underneath, in lower-case type, 'Freelance assassin mainly
under KGB control through DSS, Havana, Cuba, but often as
an independent operator for other organizations, in the
Caribbean and Central American states. Has caused wide-
spread damage, particularly to the SS, but also to CIA and
other friendly services, by murder and scientific maiming,
since 1959, the year when Castro came to power and which
seems also to have been the trigger for Scaramanga's operations. Is widely feared and admired in said territory throughout which he appears, despite police precautions, to have
complete freedom of access. Has thus become something of
a local myth and is known in his "territory" as "The Man
with the Golden Gun"—a reference to his main weapon
which is a gold-plated, long-barrelled, single-action Colt .45.
He uses special bullets with a heavy, soft (24 ct) gold core jack-
eted with silver and cross-cut at the tip, on the dum-dum prin-
ciple, for maximum wounding effect. Himself loads and
artifices this ammunition. Is responsible for the death of 267
(British Guiana), 398 (Trinidad), 943 (Jamaica) and 768 and
742 (Havana) and for the maiming and subsequent retirement
from the SS, of 098, Area Inspection Officer, by bullet wounds
in both knees. (See above references in Central Records for
Scaramanga's victims in Martinique, Haiti and Panama.)

'DESCRIPTION: Age about 35. Height 6 ft. 3 in. Slim and
fit. Eyes, light brown. Hair reddish in a crew cut. Long side-
burns. Gaunt, sombre face with thin "pencil" moustache,
brownish. Ears very flat to the head. Ambidextrous. Hands
very large and powerful and immaculately manicured. Dis-
tinguishing marks: a third nipple about two inches below his

left breast. (NB in Voodoo and allied local cults this is considered a sign of invulnerability and great sexual prowess.) Is an insatiable but indiscriminate womanizer who invariably has sexual intercourse shortly before a killing in the belief that it improves his "eye". (NB a belief shared by many professional lawn tennis players, golfers, gun and rifle marksmen and others.)

'ORIGINS: A relative of the Catalan family of circus managers of the same name with whom he spent his youth. Self-educated. At the age of 16, after the incident described below, emigrated illegally to the United States where he lived a life of petty crime on the fringes of the gangs until he graduated as a full-time gunman for the "Spangled Mob" in Nevada with the cover of pitboy in the casino of the Tiara Hotel in Las Vegas where in fact he acted as executioner of cheats and other transgressors within and outside "The Mob". In 1958 was forced to flee the States as the result of a famous duel against his opposite number for the Detroit Purple Gang, a certain Ramon "The Rod" Rodriguez, which took place by moonlight on the third green of the Thunderbird golf course at Las Vegas. (Scaramanga got two bullets into the heart of his opponent before the latter had fired a shot. Distance 20 paces.) Believed to have been compensated by "The Mob" with 100,000 dollars. Travelled the whole Caribbean area investing fugitive funds for various Las Vegas interests and later, as his reputation for keen and successful dealing in real estate and plantations became consolidated, for Trujillo of Dominica and Batista of Cuba. In 1959 settled in Havana and, seeing the way the wind blew, while remaining ostensibly a Batista man, began working undercover for the Castro party and, after the revolution, obtained an influential post as foreign "enforcer" for the DSS. In this capacity, on behalf, that is, of the Cuban Secret Police, he undertook the assassinations mentioned above.

'PASSPORTS: Various, including Cuban diplomatic.

'DISGUISES: None. They are not necessary. The myth surrounding this man, the equivalent, let us say, of that surrounding the most famous film star, and the fact that he has no police record, have hitherto given him complete freedom of movement and indemnity from interference in "his" territory. In most of the islands and mainland republics which constitute this territory, he has groups of admirers (e.g. the Rastafari in Jamaica) and commands powerful pressure groups who give him protection and succour when called upon to do so. Moreover, as the ostensible purchaser, and usually the legal front, for the "hot money" properties mentioned above, he has legitimate access, frequently supported by his diplomatic status, to any part of his territory.

'RESOURCES: Considerable but of unknown extent. Travels on various credit cards of the Diners' Club variety. He has a numbered account with the Union des Banques de Crédit, Zurich, and appears to have no difficulty in obtaining foreign currency from the slim resources of Cuba when he needs it.

'MOTIVATION: (Comment by C. C.)—' M refilled and relit his pipe, which had died. What had gone before was routine information which added nothing to his basic knowledge of the man. What followed would be of more interest. 'C. C.' covered the identity of a former Regius Professor of History at Oxford who lived a—to M—pampered existence at Headquarters in a small and, in M's opinion, over-comfortable office. In between, again in M's opinion, over-luxurious and over-long meals at the Garrick Club, he wandered, at his ease, into Headquarters, examined such files as the present one, asked questions and had signals of inquiry sent, and then delivered his judgement. But M, for all his prejudices against the man, his haircut, the casualness of his clothes, what he knew of his way of life, and the apparently haphazard processes of his ratiocination, appreciated the sharpness of the mind, the knowledge of the world, that C. C. brought to his task and, so often, the accuracy of his judgements. In short, M always enjoyed what C. C. had to say and he now picked up the file again with relish.

'I am interested in this man,' wrote C. C., 'and I have caused inquiries to be made on a somewhat wider front than usual, since it is not common to be confronted with a secret agent who is at once so much of a public figure and yet appears to be infinitely successful in the difficult and dangerous field of his choice—that of being, in common parlance, "a gun for hire". I think I may have found the origin of this partiality for killing his fellow men in cold blood, men against whom he has no personal animosity but merely the reflected animosity of his employers, in the following bizarre anecdote from his youth. In the travelling circus of his father, Enrico Scaramanga, the boy had several roles. He was a most spectacular trick shot, he was a stand-in strong man in the acrobatic troupe often taking the place of the usual artiste as bottom man in the "human pyramid" act, and he was the mahout, in gorgeous turban, Indian robes, etc., who rode the leading elephant in a troupe of three. This elephant, by the name of Max, was a male and it is a peculiarity of the male elephant, which I have learned with much interest and verified with eminent zoologists, that, at intervals during the year, they go "on heat" sexually. During these periods, a mucous deposit forms behind the animals' ears and this needs to be scraped off since otherwise it causes the

elephant intense irritation. Max developed this symptom
during a visit of the circus to Trieste, but, through an over-
sight, the condition was not noticed and given the necessary
treatment. The "Big Top" of the circus had been erected on
the outskirts of the town adjacent to the coastal railway line
and, on the night which was, in my opinion, to determine
the future way of life of the young Scaramanga, Max went
berserk, threw the youth and, screaming horrifically, trampled his way through the auditorium, causing many casual-
ties, and charged off across the fairground and on to the
railway line down which (a frightening spectacle under the
full moon which, as newspaper cuttings record, was shining
on that night) he galloped at full speed. The local carabiniere
were alerted and set off in pursuit by car along the main road
that flanks the railway line. In due course they caught up
with the unfortunate monster, which, its frenzy expired,
stood peacefully facing back the way it had come. Not real-
izing that the elephant, if approached by its handler, could
now be led peacefully back to its stall, the police opened
rapid fire and bullets from their carbines and revolvers
wounded the animal superficially in many places. Infuriated
afresh, the miserable beast, now pursued by the police car
from which the hail of fire continued, charged off again
along the railway line. On arrival at the fairground, the elephant seemed to recognize its "home", the "Big Top", and,
turning off the railway line, lumbered back through the flee-
ing spectators to the centre of the deserted arena and there,
weakened by loss of blood, pathetically continued with its
interrupted act. Trumpeting dreadfully in its agony, the mor-
tally wounded Max endeavoured again and again to raise itself and stand upon one leg. Meanwhile the young Scaramanga,
now armed with his pistols, tried to throw a lariat over the

animal's head while calling out the "elephant talk" with which he usually controlled him. Max seems to have recognized the youth and—it must have been a truly pitiful sight—lowered its trunk to allow the youth to be hoisted to his usual seat behind the elephant's head. But at this moment the police burst into the sawdust ring and their captain, approaching very close, emptied his revolver into the elephant's right eye at a range of a few feet, upon which Max fell dying to the ground. Upon this, the young Scaramanga who, according to the Press, had a deep devotion for his charger, drew one of his pistols and shot the policeman through the heart and fled off into the crowd of bystanders pursued by the other policemen who could not fire because of the throng of people. He made good his escape, found his way south to Naples and thence, as noted above, stowed away to America.

'Now, I see in this dreadful experience a possible reason for the transformation of Scaramanga into the most vicious gunman of recent years. In him was, I believe, born on that day a cold-blooded desire to avenge himself on all humanity. That the elephant had run amok and trampled many innocent people, that the man truly responsible was his handler and that the police were only doing their duty, would be, psychopathologically, either forgotten or deliberately suppressed by a youth of hot-blooded stock whose subconscious had been so deeply lacerated. At all events, Scaramanga's subsequent career requires some explanation, and I trust I am not being fanciful in putting forward my own prognosis from the known facts.'

M rubbed the bowl of his pipe thoughtfully down the side of his nose. Well, fair enough! He turned back to the file.

'I have comment,' wrote C. C., 'to make on this man's alleged sexual potency when seen in relation to his profession. It is a Freudian thesis, with which I am inclined to agree, that the pistol, whether in the hands of an amateur or of a professional gunman, has significance for the owner as a symbol of virility—an extension of the male organ—and that excessive interests in guns (e.g. gun collections and gun clubs) is a form of fetishism. The partiality of Scaramanga for a particularly showy variation of weapon, and his use of silver and gold bullets, clearly point, I think, to his being a slave to this fetish and, if I am right, I have doubts about his alleged sexual prowess, for the lack of which his gun fetish would be either a substitute or a compensation. I have also noted, from a "profile" of this man in *Time* magazine, one fact which supports my thesis that Scaramanga may be sexually abnormal. In listing his accomplishments, *Time* notes, but does not comment upon, the fact that this man cannot whistle. Now it may only be myth, and it is certainly not medical science, but there is a popular theory that a man who cannot whistle has homosexual tendencies. (At this point, the reader may care to experiment and, from his self-knowledge, help to prove or disprove this item of folklore! C. C.)' (M hadn't whistled since he was a boy. Unconsciously his mouth pursed and a clear note was emitted. He uttered an impatient 'tchah!' and continued with his reading.) 'So I would not be surprised to learn that Scaramanga is not the Casanova of popular fancy. Passing to the wider implications of gunmanship, we enter the realms of the Adlerian power urge as compensation for the inferiority complex, and here I will quote some well-turned phrases of a certain Mr Harold L. Peterson in his preface to his finely illustrated *The Book of the Gun*, published by Paul Hamlyn. Mr Peterson writes: 'In the vast array of things man has invented to better his condition, few have fascinated him more than the gun. Its function is simple; as Oliver Winchester said, with Nineteenth Century complacency, 'A gun is a machine for throwing balls.' But its ever-increasing efficiency in performing this task, and its awesome ability to strike home from long range, have given it tremendous psychological appeal.

' "For possession of a gun and the skill to use it enormously augments the gunner's personal power, and extends the radius of his influence and effect a thousand times beyond his arm's length. And since strength resides in the gun, the man who wields it may be less than strong without being disadvantaged. The flashing sword, the couched lance, the bent longbow performed to the limit of the man who held it. The gun's power is inherent and needs only to be released. A steady eye and an accurate aim are enough. Wherever the muzzle points the bullet goes, bearing the gunner's wish or intention swiftly to the target . . . Perhaps more than any other implement, the gun has shaped the course of nations and the destiny of men." '

C. C. commented: 'In the Freudian thesis, "his arm's length" would become the length of the masculine organ. But we need not linger over these esoterica. The support for my premise is well expressed in Mr Peterson's sinewy prose and, though I would substitute the printing press for the gun in his concluding paragraph, his points are well taken. The subject, Scaramanga, is, in my opinion, a paranoiac in subconscious revolt against the father figure (i.e. the figure of authority) and a sexual fetishist with possible homosexual tendencies. He has other qualities which are self-evident from the earlier testimony. In conclusion, and having regard to the damage he has already wrought upon the personnel of the SS, I conclude that his career should be terminated with the utmost dispatch—if necessary by the inhuman means he himself employs, in the unlikely event an agent of equal courage and dexterity can be made available.' Signed 'C. C.'

Beneath, at the end of the docket, the Head of the Caribbean and Central American Section had minuted 'I concur', signed 'CA', and the Chief of Staff had added, in red ink, 'Noted. COS'

M gazed into space for perhaps five minutes. Then he reached for his pen and, in green ink, scrawled the word 'Action?' followed by the italic, authoritative *M*'.

Then he sat very still for another five minutes and wondered if he had signed James Bond's death warrant.

There are few less prepossessing places to spend a hot afternoon than Kingston International Airport in Jamaica. All the money has been spent on lengthening the runway out into the harbour to take the big jets and little was left over for the comfort of transit passengers. James Bond had come in an hour before on a BWIA flight from Trinidad and there were two hours to go before his connection with a Cuban Airways flight for Havana. He had taken off his coat and tie and now sat on a hard bench gloomily surveying the contents of the In-Bond shop with its expensive scents, liquor and piles of over-decorated native ware. He had had luncheon on the plane, it was the wrong time for a drink and it was too hot and too far to take a taxi into Kingston even had he wanted to. He wiped his already soaking handkerchief over his face and neck and cursed softly and fluently.

A cleaner ambled in and, with the exquisite languor of such people throughout the Caribbean, proceeded to sweep very small bits of rubbish hither and thither, occasionally dipping a boneless hand into a bucket to sprinkle water over the dusty cement floor. Through the slatted jalousies a small breeze, reeking of the mangrove swamps, briefly stirred the dead air and then was gone. There were only two other passengers in the 'lounge', Cubans perhaps, with jippa-jappa luggage. A man and a woman. They sat close together against the opposite wall and stared fixedly at James Bond, adding minutely to the oppression of the atmosphere. Bond got up and went over to the shop. He bought a *Daily Gleaner* and returned to his place. Because of its inconsequence and occasionally bizarre choice of news the *Gleaner* was a favourite paper of Bond's. Almost the whole of that day's front page was taken up with new ganja laws to prevent the consumption, sale and cultivation of this local version of marijuana. The fact that de Gaulle had just sensationally announced his recognition of Red China was boxed well down the page. Bond read the whole paper—'country newsbits' and all— with the minute care bred of desperation. His horoscope said: 'CHEER UP! Today will bring a pleasant surprise and the fulfilment of a dear wish. But you must earn your good fortune by watching closely for the golden opportunity when it presents itself and then seizing it with both hands.' Bond smiled grimly. He would be unlikely to get on the scent of Scaramanga on his first evening in Havana. It was not even certain that Scaramanga was there. This was a last resort. For six weeks, Bond had been chasing his man round the Caribbean and Central America. He had missed him by a day in Trinidad and by only a matter of hours in Caracas. Now he had rather reluctantly taken the decision to try and ferret him out on his home ground, a particularly inimical home ground, with which Bond was barely familiar. At least he had fortified himself in British Guiana with a diplomatic passport and he was now 'Courier' Bond with splendidly engraved instructions from Her Majesty to pick up the Ja-

maican diplomatic bag in Havana and return with it. He had
even borrowed an example of the famous Silver Greyhound,
the British Courier's emblem for three hundred years. If he
could do his job and then get a few hundred yards start, this
would at least give him sanctuary in the British Embassy.
Then it would be up to the FO to bargain him out. If he could
find his man. If he could carry out his instructions. If he
could get away from the scene of the shooting. If, if, if . . .
Bond turned to the advertisements on the back page. At once
an item caught his eye. It was so typically 'old' Jamaica. This
is what he read:

FOR SALE BY AUCTION

AT 77 HARBOUR STREET, KINGSTON,
At 10.30 am on WEDNESDAY
28th MAY

under Powers of Sale contained in a mortgage from
Cornelius Brown *et ux*

No. 3½ LOVE LANE,
SAVANNAH LA MAR.

Containing the substantial residence and all that parcel of
land by measurement on the Northern Boundary three chains
and five perches, on the Southern Boundary five chains and
one perch, on the Eastern Boundary two chains exactly and
on the Western Boundary four chains and two perches be the
same in each case and more or less and butting Northerly on
No. 4 Love Lane.

THE C. D. ALEXANDER
CO. LTD.

77 HARBOUR STREET KINGSTON
PHONE 4897.

James Bond was delighted. He had had many assignments in Jamaica and many adventures on the island. The splendid address and all the stuff about chains and perches and the old-fashioned abracadabra at the end of the advertisement brought back all the authentic smell of one of the oldest and most romantic of former British possessions. For all her new-found 'Independence' he would bet his bottom dollar that the statue of Queen Victoria in the centre of Kingston had not been destroyed or removed to a museum as similar relics of an historic infancy had been in the resurgent African states. He looked at his watch. The *Gleaner* had consumed a whole hour for him. He picked up his coat and brief-case. Not much longer to go! In the last analysis, life wasn't all that dismal. One must forget the bad and remember the good. What were a couple of hours of heat and boredom in this island compared with memories of Beau Desert and Honeychile Rider and his survival against the mad Dr No? James Bond smiled to himself as the dusty pictures clicked across his brain. How long ago it all was! What had happened to her? She never wrote. The last he had heard, she had had two children by the Philadelphia doctor she had married. He wandered off into the grandly named 'Concourse' where the booths of many airlines stood empty, and promotion folders and little company flags on their counters gathered the dust blown in with the mangrove breeze.

There was the customary central display-stand holding messages for incoming and outgoing passengers. As usual, Bond wondered whether there would be something for him. In all his life there never had been. Automatically he ran his eye over the scattered envelopes, held, under tape, beneath each parent letter. Nothing under 'B' and nothing under his alias 'H' for 'Hazard, Mark' of the 'Transworld Consortium',

successor to the old 'Universal Export', that had recently
been discarded as cover for the Secret Service. Nothing. He
ran a bored eye over the other envelopes. He suddenly
froze. He looked around him, languidly, casually. The
Cuban couple were out of sight. Nobody else was looking.
He reached out a quick hand, wrapped in his handkerchief,
and pocketed the buff envelope that said, 'Scaramanga.
BOAC passenger from Lima'. He stayed where he was for a
few minutes and then wandered slowly off to the door
marked 'Men'.

He locked the door and sat down. The envelope was not
sealed. It contained a BWIA message form. The neat BWIA
writing said: 'Message received from Kingston at 12.15: the
samples will be available at No. 3½ SLM as from midday tomorrow.' There was no signature. Bond uttered a short bark
of laughter and triumph. SLM—Savannah La Mar. Could it
be? It must be! At last the three red stars of a jackpot had
clicked into line. What was it his *Gleaner* horoscope had
said? Well, he would go nap on this clue from outer space—
seize it with both hands as the *Gleaner* had instructed. He
read the message again and carefully put it back in the envelope. His damp handkerchief had left marks on the buff envelope. In this heat they would dry out in a matter of
minutes. He went out and sauntered over to the stand. There
was no one in sight. He slipped the message back into its
place under 'S' and walked over to the Cuban Airlines booth
and cancelled his reservation. He then went to the BOAC
counter and looked through the timetable. Yes, the Lima
flight for Kingston, New York and London was due in at
13.15 the next day. He was going to need help. He remembered the name of Head of Station J. He went over to the telephone booth and got through to the High Commissioner's

Office. He asked for Commander Ross. After a moment a girl's voice came on the line. 'Commander Ross's assistant. Can I help you?'

There was something vaguely familiar in the lilt of the voice. Bond said, 'Could I speak to Commander Ross? This is a friend from London.'

The girl's voice became suddenly alert. 'I'm afraid Commander Ross is away from Jamaica. Is there anything I can do?' There was a pause. 'What name did you say?'

'I didn't say any name. But in fact it's . . .'

The voice broke in excitedly, 'Don't tell me. It's James!'

Bond laughed. 'Well I'm damned! It's Goodnight! What the hell are you doing here?'

'More or less what I used to do for you. I heard you were back, but I thought you were ill or something. How absolutely marvellous! But where are you talking from?'

'Kingston Airport. Now listen, darling. I need help. We can talk later. Can you get cracking?'

'Of course. Wait till I get a pencil. Right.'

'First I need a car. Anything that'll go. Then I want the name of the top man at Frome, you know, the WISCO estate beyond Savannah La Mar. Large-scale survey map of that area, a hundred pounds in Jamaican money. Then be an angel and ring up Alexander's the auctioneers and find out anything you can about a property that's advertised in today's *Gleaner*. Say you're a prospective buyer. Three and a half Love Lane. You'll see the details. Then I want you to come out to Morgan's Harbour where I'm going in a minute, be staying the night there, and we'll have dinner and swop secrets until the dawn steals over the Blue Mountains. Can do?'

'Of course. But that's the hell of a lot of secrets. What shall I wear?'

'Something that's tight in the right places. Not too many buttons.'

She laughed. 'You've established your identity. Now I'll get on with all this. See you about seven. 'Bye.'

Gasping for air, James Bond pushed his way out of the little sweat box. He ran his handkerchief over his face and neck. He'd be damned! Mary Goodnight, his darling secretary from the old days in the OO Section! At Headquarters they had said she was abroad. He hadn't asked any questions. Perhaps she had opted for a change when he had gone missing. Anyway, what a break! Now he'd got an ally, someone he knew. Good old *Gleaner*! He got his bag from the Cuban Airlines booth and went out and hailed a taxi and said 'Morgan's Harbour' and sat back and let the air from the open windows begin to dry him.

The romantic little hotel is on the site of Port Royal at the tip of the Palisadoes. The proprietor, an Englishman who had once been in Intelligence himself and who guessed what Bond's job was, was glad to see him. He showed Bond to a comfortable air-conditioned room with a view of the pool and the wide mirror of Kingston harbour. He said, 'What is it this time? Cubans or smuggling? They're the popular targets these days.'

'Just on my way through. Got any lobsters?'

'Of course.'

'Be a good chap and save two for dinner. Broiled with melted butter. And a pot of that ridiculously expensive foie gras of yours. All right?'

'Wilco. Celebration? Champagne on the ice?'

'Good idea. Now I must get a shower and some sleep. That Kingston Airport's murder.'

James Bond woke at six. At first he didn't know where he

was. He lay and remembered. Sir James Molony had said
that his memory would be sluggish for a while. The ECT
treatment at The Park, a discreet so-called 'convalescent
home' in a vast mansion in Kent, had been fierce. Twenty-
four bashes at his brain from the black box in thirty days.
After it was over, Sir James had confessed that, if he had
been practising in America, he wouldn't have been allowed
to administer more than eighteen. At first, Bond had been
terrified at the sight of the box and of the two cathodes that
would be cupped to each temple. He had heard that people
undergoing shock treatment had to be strapped down, that
their jerking, twitching bodies, impelled by the volts, often
hurtled off the operating-table. But that, it seemed, was old
hat. Now there was the longed-for needle with the pentothol,
and Sir James said there was no movement of the body when
the current flashed through except a slight twitching of the
eyelids. And the results had been miraculous. After the
pleasant, quiet-spoken analyst had explained to him what
had been done to him in Russia, and after he had passed
through the mental agony of knowing what he had nearly
done to M, the old fierce hatred of the KGB and all its works
had been reborn in him and, six weeks after he had entered
The Park, all he wanted was to get back at the people who
had invaded his brain for their own murderous purposes.
And then had come his physical rehabilitation and the inex-
plicable amount of gun practice he had had to do at the
Maidstone police range. And then the day arrived when the
Chief of Staff had come down and explained about the gun
practice and had spent the day with him and given him his
orders, the scribble of green ink, signed 'M', that wished him
luck, and then the excitement of the ride to London Airport
on his way across the world.

Bond took another shower and dressed in shirt, slacks and sandals and wandered over to the little bar on the waterfront and ordered a double Walker's de Luxe Bourbon on the rocks and watched the pelicans diving for their dinner. Then he had another drink with a water chaser to break it down and wondered about 3½ Love Lane and what the 'samples' would consist of and how he would take Scaramanga. This had been worrying him since he had been given his orders. It was all very fine to be told to 'eliminate' the man, but James Bond had never liked killing in cold blood and to provoke a draw against a man who was possibly the fastest gun in the world was suicide. Well, he would just have to see which way the cards fell. The first thing to do was to clean up his cover. The diplomatic passport he would leave with Goodnight. He would now be 'Mark Hazard' of the 'Transworld Consortium', the splendidly vague title which could cover almost any kind of human activity. His business would have to be with the West Indies Sugar Company because that was the only business, apart from Kaiser Bauxite, that existed in the comparatively deserted western districts of Jamaica. There was also the Negril project for developing one of the most spectacular beaches in the world, beginning with the building of the Thunderbird Hotel. He could be a rich man looking around for a building site. If his hunch was right, and the childish predictions of his horoscope, and if he came up with Scaramanga at the romantic Love Lane address, it would be a question of playing it by ear.

The prairie fire of the sunset raged briefly in the west and the molten sea cooled off into moonlit gun-metal.

A naked arm smelling of Chanel No. 5 snaked round his neck and warm lips kissed the corner of his mouth. As he reached up to hold the arm where it was, a breathless voice said, 'Oh, James! I'm sorry. I just had to! It's so wonderful to have you back.'

Bond put his hand under the soft chin and lifted up her mouth and kissed her full on the half-open lips. He said, 'Why didn't we ever think of doing that before, Goodnight? Three years with only that door between us! What must we have been thinking of?'

She stood away from him. The golden bell of hair fell back to embrace her neck. She hadn't changed. Still only the faintest trace of make-up, but now the face was golden with sunburn from which the wide-apart blue eyes, now ablaze with the moon, shone out with that challenging directness that had disconcerted him when they had argued over some office problem. Still the same glint of health over the good bones and the broad uninhibited smile from the full lips that, in repose, were so exciting. But now the clothes were different. Instead of the severe shirt and skirt of the days at Headquarters, she was wearing a single string of pearls and a one-piece short-skirted frock in the colour of a pink gin with a lot of bitters in it—the orangey-pink of the inside of a conch shell. It was all tight against the bosom and the hips. She smiled at his scrutiny. 'The buttons are down the back. This is standard uniform for a tropical Station.'

'I can just see Q Branch dreaming it up. I suppose one of the pearls has a death pill in it.'

'Of course. But I can't remember which. I'll just have to swallow the whole string. Can I have a daiquiri, please, instead?'

Bond gave the order. 'Sorry, Goodnight. My manners are slipping. I was dazzled. It's so tremendous finding you here. And I've never seen you in your working clothes before. Now then, tell me the news. Where's Ross? How long have

you been here? Have you managed to cope with all that junk
I gave you?'

Her drink came. She sipped it carefully. Bond remembered
that she rarely drank and didn't smoke. He ordered another
for himself and felt vaguely guilty that this was his third
double and that she wouldn't know it and when it came
wouldn't recognize it as a double. He lit a cigarette. Nowa-
days he was trying to keep to twenty and failing by about
five. He stabbed the cigarette out. He was getting near to his
target and the rigid training rules that had been drilled into
him at The Park must from now on be observed meticu-
lously. The champagne wouldn't count. He was amused by
the conscience this girl had awakened in him. He was also
surprised and impressed.

Mary Goodnight knew that the last question was the one
he would want answered first. She reached into a plain
straw handbag on a gold metal chain and handed him a thick
envelope. She said, 'Mostly in used singles. A few fivers.
Shall I debit you direct or put it in as expenses?'

'Direct, please.'

'The car's outside. You remember Strangways? Well it's his
old Sunbeam Alpine. The Station bought it and now I use it.
The tank's full and it goes like a bird. The top man at Frome
is a man called Tony Hugill. Ex-navy. Nice man. Nice wife.
Nice children. Does a good job. Has a lot of trouble with cane
burning and other small sabotage—mostly with thermite
bombs brought in from Cuba. Cuba's sugar crop is Jamaica's
chief rival and with Hurricane Flora and all the rains they've
been having over there, the Cuban crop is going to be only
about three million tons this year, compared with a Batista
level of about seven, and very late, because the rains have
played havoc with the sucrose content.' She smiled her wide

smile. 'No secrets. Just reading the *Gleaner*. So it's worth Castro's trouble to try and keep the world price up by doing as much damage as he can to rival crops so that he's in a better position to bargain with Russia. He's only got his sugar to sell and he wants food badly. This wheat the Americans are selling to Russia. A lot of that will find its way back to Cuba, in exchange for sugar, to feed the Cuban sugar croppers.' She smiled again. 'Pretty daft business, isn't it? I don't think Castro can hold out much longer. The missile business in Cuba must have cost Russia about a billion pounds. And now they're having to pour money into Cuba, money and goods, to keep the place on its feet. I can't help thinking they'll pull out soon and leave Castro to go the way Batista went. It's a fiercely Catholic country and Hurricane Flora was considered as the final judgement from heaven. It sat over the island and simply whipped it, day after day, for five days. No hurricane in history has ever behaved like that. The churchgoers don't miss an omen like that. It was a straight indictment of the regime.'

Bond said with admiration, 'Goodnight, you're a treasure. You've certainly been doing your homework.'

The direct blue eyes looked straight into his, dodging the compliment. 'This is the stuff I live with here. It's built into the Station. But I thought you might like some background to Frome and what I've said explains why WISCO are getting these cane fires. At least we think it is. Apparently there's a tremendous chess game going on all over the world in sugar—in what they call sugar futures, that's sort of buying the stuff forward for delivery dates later in the year. Washington's trying to keep the price down, to upset Cuba's economy, but there's increased world consumption and a shortage largely due to Flora and the tremendous rains we've been having here after Flora which have delayed the Jamaican crop. I don't understand it all, but it's in Cuba's interest to do as much damage as possible to the Jamaican crop and this place Frome you're interested in produces about a quarter of Jamaica's total output.' She took a sip at her drink. 'Well, that's all about sugar. The top man there is this man Hugill. We've had a lot to do with him, so he'll be friendly. He was in Naval Intelligence during the war, sort of commando job, so he knows the score. The car's a bit aged but it's still pretty fast and it won't let you down. It's rather bashed about so it won't be conspicuous. I've put the survey map in the glove compartment.'

'That's fine. Now, last question and then we'll go and have dinner and tell each other our life stories. But, by the way, what's happened to your chief, Ross?'

Mary Goodnight looked worried. 'To tell you the truth, I don't exactly know. He went off last week on some job in Trinidad. It was to try and locate a man called Scaramanga. He's a local gunman of some sort. I don't know much about him. Apparently Headquarters want him traced for some reason.' She smiled ruefully. 'Nobody ever tells me anything that's interesting. I just do the donkey work. Well, Commander Ross was due back two days ago and he hasn't turned up. I've had to send off a Red Warning, but I've been told to give him another week.'

'Well, I'm glad he's out of the way. I'd rather have his Number Two. Last question. What about this 3½ Love Lane? Did you get anywhere?'

Mary Goodnight blushed. 'Did I not! That was a fine question to get me mixed up with. Alexander's were non-committal and I finally had to go to the Special Branch. I shan't be able to show my face there for weeks. Heaven

knows what they must think of you. That place is a, is a, er—'
She wrinkled her nose. 'It's a famous disorderly house in
Sav' La Mar.'

Bond laughed out loud at her discomfiture. He teased her
with malicious but gentle sadism. 'You mean it's a whore-
house?'

'James! For heaven's sake! Must you be so crude?'

The south coast of Jamaica is not as beautiful as the north, and it is a long 120-mile hack over very mixed road surfaces from Kingston to Savannah La Mar. Mary Goodnight had insisted on coming along, 'to navigate and help with the punctures'. Bond had not demurred.

Spanish Town, May Pen, Alligator Pond, Black River, Whitehouse Inn, where they had luncheon—the miles unrolled under the fierce sun until, around four in the afternoon, a stretch of good straight road brought them among the spruce little villas, each with its patch of brownish lawn, bougainvillaea, and single bed of canna lilies and crotons, which make up the 'smart' suburbs of the modest little coastal township that is, in the vernacular, Sav' La Mar.

Except for the old quarter on the waterfront, it is not a typically Jamaican town, nor a very attractive one. The villas, built for the senior staff of the Frome sugar estates, are drably respectable, and the small straight streets smack of a most un-Jamaican bout of town planning around the 1920s. Bond stopped at the first garage, took in petrol and put Mary Goodnight into a hired car for the return trip. He had told her

nothing of his assignment and she had asked no questions
when Bond told her vaguely that it was 'something to do
with Cuba'. Bond said he would keep in touch when he
could, and get back to her when his job was done and then,
businesslike, she was off back down the dusty road and
Bond drove slowly down to the waterfront. He identified
Love Lane, a narrow street of broken-down shops and houses
that meandered back into the town from the jetty. He circled
the area to get the neighbouring geography clear in his mind
and parked the car in a deserted area near the spit of sand on
which fishing canoes were drawn up on raised stilts. He
locked the car and sauntered back and into Love Lane. There
were a few people about, poor people of the fisherman class.
Bond bought a packet of Royal Blend at a small general store
that smelled of spices. He asked where No. 3½ was and got a
look of polite curiosity. 'Further up de street. Mebbe a chain.
Big house on de right.' Bond moved over to the shady side
and strolled on. He slit open the packet with his thumbnail
and lit a cigarette to help the picture of an idle tourist examining a corner of old Jamaica. There was only one big house
on the right. He took some time lighting the cigarette while
he examined it.

It must once have had importance, perhaps as the private
house of a merchant. It was of two storeys with balconies
running all the way round and it was wooden built with sil-
vering shingles, but the gingerbread tracery beneath the
eaves was broken in many places and there was hardly a
scrap of paint left on the jalousies that closed off all the upstairs windows and most of those below. The patch of 'yard'
bordering the street was inhabited by a clutch of vulturine-
necked chickens that pecked at nothing and three skeletal Jamaican black-and-tan mongrels. They gazed lazily across the

street at Bond and scratched and bit at invisible flies. But, in the background, there was one very beautiful *lignum vitae* tree in full blue blossom. Bond guessed that it was as old as the house—perhaps fifty years. It certainly owned the property by right of strength and adornment. In its delicious black shade a girl in a rocking chair sat reading a magazine. At the range of about thirty yards she looked tidy and pretty. Bond strolled up the opposite side of the street until a corner of the house hid the girl. Then he stopped and examined the house more closely.

Wooden steps ran up to an open front door, over whose lintel, whereas few of the other buildings in the street bore numbers, a big enamelled metal sign announced '3½' in white on dark blue. Of the two broad windows that bracketed the door, the left-hand one was shuttered, but the right-hand one was a single broad sheet of rather dusty glass through which tables and chairs and a serving-counter could be seen. Over the door a swinging sign said 'Dreamland Cafe' in sun-bleached letters, and round this window were advertisements for Red Stripe beer, Royal Blend, Four Aces cigarettes and Coca-Cola. A hand-painted sign said 'SNAX' and, underneath, 'Hot Cock Soup Fresh Daily.'

Bond walked across the street and up the steps and parted the bead curtain that hung over the entrance. He walked over to the counter and was inspecting its contents, a plate of dry-looking ginger cakes, a pile of packeted banana crisps, and some sweet jars, when he heard quick steps outside. The girl from the garden came in. The beads clashed softly behind her. She was an octoroon, pretty as, in Bond's imagination, the word octoroon suggested. She had bold, brown eyes, slightly uptilted at the corners, beneath a fringe of silken black hair. (Bond reflected that there would be Chinese blood somewhere in her past.) She was dressed in a short frock of shocking pink which went well with the coffee and cream of her skin. Her wrists and ankles were tiny. She smiled politely. The eyes flirted. 'Evenin'.'

'Good evening. Could I have a Red Stripe?'

'Sure.' She went behind the counter. She gave him a quick glimpse of fine bosoms as she bent to the door of the icebox—a glimpse not dictated by the geography of the place. She nudged the door shut with a knee, deftly uncapped the bottle and put it on the counter beside an almost clean glass. 'That'll be one and six.'

Bond paid. She rang the money into the cash register. Bond drew up a stool to the counter and sat down. She rested her arms on the wooden top and looked across at him. 'Passing through?'

'More or less. I saw this place was for sale in yesterday's *Gleaner*. I thought I'd take a look at it. Nice big house. Does it belong to you?'

She laughed. It was a pity, because she was a pretty girl, but the teeth had been sharpened by munching raw sugar cane. 'What a hope! I'm sort of, well sort of manager. There's the café' (she pronounced it caif) 'and mebbe you heard we got other attractions.'

Bond looked puzzled. 'What sort?'

'Girls. Six bedrooms upstairs. Very clean. It only cost a pound. There's Sarah up there now. Care to meet up with her?'

'Not today, thanks. It's too hot. But you only have one at a time?'

'There's Lindy, but she's engaged. She's a big girl. If you like them big, she'll be free in half an hour.' She glanced at the kitchen clock on the wall behind her. 'Around six o'clock. It'll be cooler then.'

'I prefer girls like you. What's your name?'

She giggled. 'I only do it for love. I told you I just manage the place. They call me Tiffy.'

'That's an unusual name. How did you come by it?'

'My momma had six girls. Called them all after flowers. Violet, Rose, Cherry, Pansy and Lily. Then when I came, she couldn't think of any more flower names so she called me "Artificial".' Tiffy waited for him to laugh. When he didn't, she went on. 'When I went to school they all said it was a wrong name and laughed at me and shortened it to Tiffy and that's how I've stayed.'

'Well, I think it's a very pretty name. My name's Mark.'

She flirted. 'You a saint too?'

'No one's ever accused me of it. I've been up at Frome doing a job. I like this part of the island and it crossed my mind to find some place to rent. But I want to be closer to the sea than this. I'll have to look around a bit more. Do you rent rooms by the night?'

She reflected. 'Sure. Why not. But you may find it a bit noisy. There's sometimes a customer who's taken some drinks too many. And there's not too much plumbing.' She leaned closer and lowered her voice. 'But I wouldn't have advised you to rent the place. The shingles are in bad shape. Cost you mebbe five hunnerd, mebbe a thousand to get the roof done.'

'It's nice of you to tell me that. But why's the place being sold? Trouble with the police?'

'Not so much. We operate a respectable place. But in the *Gleaner*, after Mr Brown, that's my boss, you read that "et ux"?'

'Yes.'

'Well, seems that means "and his wife". And Mistress Brown, Mistress Agatha Brown, she was Church of England, but she just done gone to the Catholics. And it seems they don't hold with places like 3½, not even when they're decently run. And their church here, just up the street, seems that needs a new roof like here. So Mistress Brown figures to kill two birds with the same stone and she goes on at Mr Brown to close the place down and sell it and with her portion she goin' fix the roof for the Catholics.'

'That's a shame. It seems a nice quiet place. What's going to happen to you?'

'Guess I'll move to Kingston. Live with one of my sisters and mebbe work in one of the big stores—Issa's mebbe, or Nathan's. Sav' La Mar is sort of quiet.' The brown eyes became introspective. 'But I'll sure miss the place. Folks have fun here and Love Lane's a pretty street. We're all friends up and down the Lane. It's got sort of, sort of . . .'

'Atmosphere.'

'Right. That's what it's got. Like sort of old Jamaica. Like it must have been in the old days. Everyone's friends with each other. Help each other when they have trouble. You'd be surprised how often the girls do it for free if the man's a good feller, regular customer sort of, and he's short.' The brown eyes gazed inquiringly at Bond to see if he understood the strength of the evidence.

'That's nice of them. But it can't be good for business.'

She laughed. 'This ain't no business, Mister Mark. Not while I'm running it. This is a public service, like water and electricity and health and education and . . .' She broke off and glanced over her shoulder at the clock which said 5.45. 'Hell! You got me talking so much I've forgot Joe and May. It's their supper.' She went to the café window and wound it down. At once, from the direction of the *lignum vitae* tree, two large black birds, slightly smaller than a raven, whirled in, circled the interior of the café amidst a metallic clangour of song unlike the song of any other bird in the world, and untidily landed on the counter within reach of Bond's hand. They strutted up and down imperiously, eyeing Bond without fear from bold, golden eyes and went through a piercing repertoire of tinny whistles and trills, some of which required them to ruffle themselves up to almost twice their normal size.

Tiffy went back behind the bar, took two pennies out of her purse, rang them up on the register and took two ginger cakes out of the flyblown display case. She broke off bits and fed the two birds, always the smaller of the two, the female, first, and they greedily seized the pieces from her fingers, and, holding the scraps to the wooden counter with a claw, tore them into smaller fragments and devoured them. When it was all over, and Tiffy had chided them both for pecking her fingers, they made small, neat white messes on the counter and looked pleased with themselves. Tiffy took a cloth and cleaned up the messes. She said, 'We call them kling-klings but learned folk call them Jamaican grackles. They're very friendly folk. The Doctor Bird, the humming bird with the streamer tail, is the Jamaican national bird, but I like these best. They're not so beautiful, but they're the friendliest birds and they're funny besides. They seem to know it. They're like naughty black thieves.' The kling-klings eyed the cake stand and complained stridently that their supper was over. James Bond produced twopence and handed it over. 'They're wonderful. Like mechanical toys. Give them a second course from me.'

Tiffy rang up the money and took out two more cakes. 'Now listen, Joe and May. This nice gemmun's been nice to Tiffy and he's now being nice to you. So don't you peck my

fingers and make messes or mebbe he won't visit us again.'
She was half-way through feeding the birds when she
cocked an ear. There was the noise of creaking boards somewhere overhead and then the sound of quiet footsteps tread-
ing stairs. All of a sudden Tiffy's animated face became quiet
and tense. She whispered to Bond: 'That's Lindy's man. Important man. He's a good customer here. But he don't like me
because I won't go with him. So he can talk rough sometimes. And he don't like Joe and May because he reckons
they make too much noise.' She shooed the birds in the direction of the open window, but they saw there was half
their cake to come and they just fluttered into the air and
then down to the counter again. Tiffy appealed to Bond. 'Be
a good friend and just sit quiet whatever he says. He likes to
get people mad. And then . . .'

She stopped. 'Will you have another Red Stripe, mister?'

Bead curtains swished in the shadowy back of the room.

Bond had been sitting with his chin propped on his right
hand. He now dropped the hand to the counter and sat back.
The Walther PPK inside the waistband of his trousers to the
left of his flat stomach signalled its presence to his skin. The
fingers of his right hand curled slightly, ready to receive its
butt. He moved his left foot off the rail of the stool on to the
floor. He said, 'That'd be fine.' He unbuttoned his coat with his
left hand and then, with the same hand, took out his handkerchief and wiped his face with it. 'It always gets extra hot
around six before the Undertaker's Wind has started to blow.'

'Mister, the undertaker's right here. You care to feel his
wind?'

James Bond turned his head slowly. Dusk had crept into
the big room and all he could see was a pale, tall outline. The
man was carrying a suitcase. He put it down on the floor and

came forward. He must have been wearing rubber-soled shoes for his feet made no sound. Tiffy moved nervously behind the counter and a switch clicked. Half a dozen low-voltage bulbs came to life in rusty brackets around the walls.

Bond said easily, 'You made me jump.'

Scaramanga came up and leant against the counter. The description in Records was exact, but it had not caught the cat-like menace of the big man, the extreme breadth of the shoulders and the narrow waist, or the cold immobility of the eyes that now examined Bond with an expression of aloof disinterest. He was wearing a well-cut, single-breasted tan suit and 'co-respondent' shoes in brown and white. Instead of a tie, he wore a high stock in white silk secured by a gold pin the shape of a miniature pistol. There should have been something theatrical about the get-up but, perhaps because of the man's fine figure, there wasn't.

He said, 'I sometimes make 'em dance. Then I shoot their feet off.' There was no trace of a foreign accent underneath the American.

Bond said, 'That sounds rather drastic. What do you do it for?'

'The last time it was five thousand dollars. Seems like you don't know who I am. Didn't the cool cat tell you?'

Bond glanced at Tiffy. She was standing very still, her hands by her sides. The knuckles were white.

Bond said, 'Why should she? Why would I want to know?'

There was a quick flash of gold. The small black hole looked directly at Bond's navel. 'Because of this. What are you doing here, stranger? Kind of a coincidence finding a city slicker at 3½. Or at Sav' La Mar for the matter of that. Not by any chance from the police? Or any of their friends?'

'Kamerad!' Bond raised his hands in mock surrender. He

lowered them and turned to Tiffy. 'Who is this man? A one-man takeover bid for Jamaica? Or a refugee from a circus? Ask him what he'd like to drink. Whoever he is, it was a good act.' James Bond knew that he had very nearly pulled the trigger of the gun. Hit a gunman in his vanity . . . He had a quick vision of himself writhing on the floor, his right hand without the power to reach for his own weapon. Tiffy's pretty face was no longer pretty. It was a taut skull. She stared at James Bond. Her mouth opened but no sound came from the gaping lips. She liked him and she knew he was dead. The kling-klings, Joe and May, smelled the same electricity. With a tremendous din of metallic squawks, they fled for the open window like black thieves escaping into the night.

The explosions from the Colt .45 were deafening. The two birds disintegrated against the violet back-drop of the dusk, the scraps of feathers and pink flesh blasting out of the yellow light of the café into the limbo of the deserted street like shrapnel.

There was a moment of deafening silence. James Bond didn't move. He sat where he was, waiting for the tension of the deed to relax. It didn't. With an inarticulate scream, that was half a filthy word, Tiffy took James Bond's bottle of Red Stripe off the counter and clumsily flung it. There came a distant crash of glass from the back of the room. Then, having made her puny gesture, Tiffy fell to her knees behind the counter and went into sobbing hysterics.

James Bond drank down the rest of his beer and got slowly to his feet. He walked towards Scaramanga and was about to pass him when the man reached out a languid left arm and caught him at the biceps. He held the snout of his gun to his nose, sniffing delicately. The expression in the dead brown eyes was far-away. He said, 'Mister, there's something quite extra about the smell of death. Care to try it?' He held out the glittering gun as if he was offering James Bond a rose.

Bond stood quite still. He said, 'Mind your manners. Take your hand off me.'

Scaramanga raised his eyebrows. The flat, leaden gaze seemed to take in Bond for the first time.

He released his grip.

James Bond went on round the edge of the counter. When he came opposite the other man, he found the eyes were now looking at him with faint, scornful curiosity. Bond stopped. The sobbing of the girl was the crying of a small dog. Somewhere down the street a 'Sound System'—a loudspeaker record player—began braying calypso.

Bond looked the man in the eye. He said, 'Thanks. I've tried it. I recommend the Berlin vintage. 1945.' He smiled a friendly, only slightly ironical smile. 'But I expect you were too young to be at that tasting.'

Bond knelt down beside Tiffy and gave her a couple of sharp slaps on the right cheek. Then on the left. The wet eyes came back into focus. She put her hand up to her face and looked at Bond with surprise. Bond got to his feet. He took a cloth and wetted it at the tap, then leant down and put his arm round her and wiped the cloth gently over her face. Then he lifted her up and handed her her bag that was on a shelf behind the counter. He said, 'Come on, Tiffy. Make up that pretty face again. Business'll be warming up soon. The leading lady's got to look her best.'

Tiffy took the bag and opened it. She looked past Bond and saw Scaramanga for the first time since the shooting. The pretty lips drew back in a snarl. She whispered fiercely so that only Bond could hear, 'I'm goin' fix that man, but good. There's Mother Edna up Orange Hill way. She's an obeah top woman. I'll go up there tomorrow. Come a few days, he won't know what hit him.' She took out a mirror and began doing up her face. Bond reached into his hip pocket and counted out five one-pound notes. He stuffed them into her open bag.

'You forget all about it. This'll buy you a nice canary in a cage to keep you company. Anyway, another pair of klings'll come along if you put some food out.' He patted her shoulder and moved away. When he came up with Scaramanga he stopped and said, 'That may have been a good circus act,' (he used the word again on purpose) 'but it was rough on the girl. Give her some money.'

Scaramanga said, 'Shove it,' out of the corner of his mouth. He said suspiciously, 'And what's all this yack about circuses?' He turned to face Bond. 'Just stop where you are, Mister, and answer a few questions. Like I said, are you from the police? You've sure got the smell of cops around you. If not, what are you doing hereabouts?'

Bond said, 'People don't tell me what to do. I tell them.' He walked on into the middle of the room and sat down at a table. He said, 'Come and sit down and stop trying to lean on me. I'm unleanable-on.'

Scaramanga shrugged. He took two long strides, picked up one of the metal chairs, twirled it round and thrust it between his legs and sat bassackwards, his left arm lying along the back of the chair. His right arm rested on his thigh, inches from the ivory pistol butt that showed above the waistband of his trousers. Bond recognized that it was a good working position for a gunman, the metal back of the chair acting as a shield for most of the body. This was certainly a most careful and professional man.

Bond, both hands in full view on the table top, said cheerfully, 'No. I'm not from the police. My name's Mark Hazard. I'm from a company called "Transworld Consortium". I've been doing a job at Frome, the WISCO sugar place. Know it?'

'Sure I know it. What you been doing there?'

'Not so fast, my friend. First of all, who are you and what's your business?'

'Scaramanga. Francisco Scaramanga. Labour relations. Ever heard of me?'

Bond frowned. 'Can't say I have? Should I have?'

'Some people who hadn't are dead.'

'A lot of people who haven't heard of me are dead.' Bond leaned back. He crossed one leg over the other, above the knee, and grasped the ankle in a clubman pose. 'I do wish you'd stop talking in heroics. For instance, seven hundred million Chinese have certainly heard of neither of us. You must be a frog in a very small pool.'

Scaramanga did not rise to the jibe. He said reflectively, 'Yeah. I guess you could call the Caribbean a pretty small pool. But there's good pickin's to be had from it. "The man with the golden gun." That's what they call me in these parts.'

'It's a handy tool for solving labour problems. We could do with you up at Frome.'

'Been having trouble up there?' Scaramanga looked bored.

'Too many cane fires.'

'Was that your business?'

'Sort of. One of the jobs of my company is insurance investigation.'

'Security work. I've come across guys like you before. Thought I could smell the cop-smell.' Scaramanga looked satisfied that his guess had been right. 'Did you get any-where?'

'Picked up a few Rastafari. I'd have liked to get rid of the lot of them. But they went crying to their union that they were being discriminated against because of their religion so we had to call a halt. So the fires'll begin again soon. That's why I say we could do with a good enforcer up there.' Bond added blandly, 'I take it that's another name for your profession?'

Again Scaramanga dodged the sneer. He said, 'You carry a gun?'

'Of course. You don't go after the Rastas without one.'

'What kind of a gun?'

'Walther PPK. 7.65 millimetre.'

'Yes, that's a stopper all right.' Scaramanga turned towards the counter. 'Hey, cool cat. Couple of Red Stripes, if you're in business again.' He turned back and the blank eyes looked hard at Bond. 'What's your next job?'

'Don't know. I'll have to contact London and find out if they've got any other problems in the area. But I'm in no hurry. I work for them more or less on a freelance basis. Why? Any suggestions?'

The other man sat quiet while Tiffy came out from behind the counter. She came over to the table and placed the tin tray with the bottles and glasses in front of Bond. She didn't look at Scaramanga. Scaramanga uttered a harsh bark of laughter. He reached inside his coat and took out an alligator-skin billfold. He extracted a hundred-dollar bill and threw it on the table. 'No hard feelings, cool cat. You'd be okay if you didn't always keep your legs together. Go buy yourself some more birds with that. I like to have smiling people around me.'

Tiffy picked up the note. She said, 'Thanks, Mister. You'd be surprised what I'm going to spend your money on.' She gave him a long, hard look and turned on her heel.

Scaramanga shrugged. He reached for a bottle of beer and a glass and both men poured and drank. Scaramanga took out an expensive cigar case, selected a pencil-thin cheroot and lit it with a match. He let the smoke dribble out between his lips and inhaled the thin stream up his nostrils. He did this several times with the same mouthful of smoke until the smoke was dissipated. All the while he stared across the table at Bond, seeming to weigh up something in his mind. He said, 'Care to earn yourself a grand—a thousand bucks?'

Bond said, 'Possibly.' He paused and added, 'Probably.' What he meant was, 'Of course! If it means staying close to you, my friend.'

Scaramanga smoked a while in silence. A car stopped outside and two laughing men came quickly up the steps. When they came through the bead curtains, working-class Jamaicans, they stopped laughing and went quietly over to the counter and began whispering to Tiffy. Then they both slapped a pound note on the counter and, making a wide detour away from the white men, disappeared through the curtains at the back of the room. Their laughter began again as Bond heard their footsteps on the stairs.

Scaramanga hadn't taken his eyes from Bond's face. Now he said, keeping his voice low, 'I got myself a problem. Some partners of mine, they've taken an interest in this Negril development. Far end of the property. Place called Bloody Bay. Know it?'

'I've seen it on the map. Just short of Green Island Harbour.'

'Right. So I've got some shares in the business. So we start building a hotel and get the first storey finished and the main living-rooms and restaurant and so on. So then the tourist boom slackens off—Americans get frightened of being so close to Cuba or some such crap. And the banks get difficult and money begins to run short. Follow me?'

'So you're a stale bull of the place?'

'Right. So I came over a few days ago and I'm staying at the Thunderbird and I've got a half-dozen of the main stockholders to fly in for a meeting on the spot. Sort of look the place over and get our heads together and figure what to do next. Now, I want to give these guys a good time so I've got a smart combo over from Kingston, calypso singers, limbo, plenty of girls—all that jazz. And there's swimming and one of the features of the place is a small-scale railway that used to handle the sugar cane. Runs to Green Island Harbour where I gotta forty-foot Chriscraft Roamer. Deep-sea fishing. That'll be another outing. Get me? Give the fellers a real good time.'

'So that they'll get all enthusiastic and buy out your share of the stock?'

Scaramanga frowned angrily. 'I'm not paying you a grand to get the wrong ideas. Or any ideas for the matter of that.'

'What for then?'

For a moment or two Scaramanga went through his smoking routine, the little pillars of smoke vanishing again and again into the black nostrils. It seemed to calm him. His forehead cleared. He said, 'Some of these men are kind of rough. We're all stockholders, of course, but that don't necessarily mean we're friends. Understand? I'll be wanting to hold some meetings, private meetings, with mebbe only two or three guys at a time, sort of sounding out the different interests. Could be that some of the other guys, the ones not invited to a particular meeting, might get it into their heads to bug a meeting or try and get wise to what goes on in one way or another. So it jes' occurs to me that you being live to security and such, that you could act as a kind of guard at these meetings, clean the room for mikes, stay outside the door and see that no one comes nosing around, see that when I want to be private I git private. D'you get the photo?'

Bond had to laugh. He said, 'So you want to hire me as a kind of personal bodyguard. Is that it?'

The frown was back. 'And what's so funny about that, Mister? It's good money, ain't it? Three, mebbe four days in a luxury joint like the Thunderbird. A thousand bucks at the end of it? What's so screwy about that proposition, eh?' Scaramanga mashed out the butt of his cigar against the underside of the table. A shower of sparks fell. He let them lie.

Bond scratched the back of his head as if reflecting. Which he was—furiously. He knew that he hadn't heard the full story. He also knew that it was odd, to say the least of it, for this man to hire a complete stranger to do this job for him. The job itself stood up, but only just. It made sense that Scaramanga would not want to hire a local man, an ex-policeman for instance, even if one could be found. Such a man might have friends in the hotel business who would be interested in the speculative side of the Negril development. And, of course, on the plus side, Bond would be achieving what he had never thought possible—he would have got right inside Scaramanga's guard. Or would he? There was the strong smell of a trap. But, assuming that Bond had not, by some obscure bit of ill luck, been blown, he couldn't for the life of him see what the trap could be. Well, clearly, he must make the gamble. In so many respects it was a chance in a million.

Bond lit a cigarette. He said, 'I was only laughing at the idea of a man of your particular skills wanting protection. But it all sounds great fun. Of course I'll come along. When do we start? I've got a car at the bottom of the road.'

Scaramanga thrust out an inside wrist and looked at a thin gold watch on a two-coloured gold bracelet. He said, '6.32. My car'll be outside.' He got up. 'Let's go. But don't forget one thing, Mister Whoosis. I rile mighty easy. Get me?'

Bond said easily, 'I saw how annoyed you got with those

inoffensive birds.' He stood up. 'I don't see any reason why either of us should get riled.'

Scaramanga said indifferently, 'Okay, then.' He walked to the back of the room and picked up his suitcase, new-looking but cheap, strode to the exit and clashed through the bead curtain and down the steps.

Bond went quickly over to the counter. 'Goodbye, Tiffy. Hope I'll be coming by again one day. If anyone should ask after me, say I'm at the Thunderbird Hotel at Bloody Bay.'

Tiffy reached out a hand and timidly touched his sleeve. 'Go careful over there, Mister Mark. There's gangster money in that place. And watch out for yourself.' She jerked her head towards the exit: 'That's the worstest man I ever heard tell of.' She leaned forward and whispered, 'That's a thousand pound worth of ganja he's got in that bag. Rasta left it for him this morning. So I smelled the bag.' She drew quickly back.

Bond said, 'Thanks, Tiffy. See Mother Edna puts a good hex on him. I'll tell you why some day. I hope. 'Bye!' He went quickly out and down into the street where a red Thunderbird convertible was waiting, its exhaust making a noise like an expensive motor-boat. The chauffeur was a Jamaican, smartly dressed, with a peaked cap. A red pennant on the wireless aerial said 'The Thunderbird Hotel' in gold. Scaramanga was sitting beside the chauffeur. He said impatiently, 'Get in the back. Lift you down to your car. Then follow along. It gets a good road after a while.'

James Bond got into the car behind Scaramanga and wondered whether to shoot the man now, in the back of the head—the old Gestapo-KGB point of puncture. A mixture of reasons prevented him—the itch of curiosity, an inbuilt dislike of cold murder, the feeling that this was not the predestined moment, the likelihood that he would have to murder the chauffeur also—these, combined with the softness of the night and the fact that the 'Sound System' was now playing a good recording of one of his favourites, 'After You've Gone', and that cicadas were singing from the *lignum vitae* tree, said 'No'. But at that moment, as the car coasted down Love Lane towards the bright mercury of the sea, James Bond knew that he was not only disobeying orders, or at best dodging them, he was also being a bloody fool.

When he arrives at a place on a dark night, particularly in an alien land which he has never seen before—a strange house, perhaps, or an hotel—even the most alert man is assailed by the confused sensations of the meanest tourist.

James Bond more or less knew the map of Jamaica. He knew that the sea had always been close to him on his left and, as he followed the twin red glares of the leading car through an impressive entrance gate of wrought iron and up an avenue of young Royal palms, he heard the waves scrolling into a beach very close to his car. The fields of sugar cane would, he guessed from the approach, come close up against the new high wall that surrounded the Thunderbird property, and there was a slight smell of mangrove swamp coming down from below the high hills whose silhouette he had occasionally glimpsed under a scudding three-quarter moon on his right. But otherwise he had no clue to exactly where he was or what sort of place he was now approaching and, particularly for him, the sensation was an uncomfortable one.

The first law for a secret agent is to get his geography right, his means of access and exit, and assure his communications with the outside world. James Bond was uncomfortably aware of that, for the past hour, he had been driving into limbo and that his nearest contact was a girl in a brothel thirty miles away. The situation was not reassuring.

Half a mile ahead, someone must have seen the approaching lights of the leading car and pressed switches, for there was a sudden blaze of brilliant yellow illumination through the trees and a final sweep of the drive revealed the hotel. With the theatrical lighting and the surrounding blackness to conceal any evidence of halted construction work, the place made a brave show. A vast pale-pink-and-white pillared portico gave the hotel an aristocratic frontage and, when Bond drew up behind the other car at the entrance, he could see through the tall Regency windows a vista of black-and-white marble flooring beneath blazing chandeliers. A bell captain and his Jamaican staff in red jackets and black trousers hurried down the steps and, after showing great deference to Scaramanga, took his suitcase and Bond's, then the small cavalcade moved into the entrance hall where Bond wrote 'Mark Hazard' and the Kensington address of Transworld Consortium in the register.

Scaramanga had been talking to a man who appeared to be the manager, a young American with a neat face and a neat suit. He turned to Bond. 'You're in Number 24 in the West Wing. I'm close by in Number 20. Order what you want from Room Service. See you about ten in the morning. The guys'll be coming in from Kingston around midday. Okay?' The cold eyes in the gaunt face didn't mind whether it was or not. Bond said it was. He followed one of the bell boys with his suitcase across the slippery marble floor and through an archway on the left of the hall and down a long white corridor with a close-fitted carpet in royal blue Wilton. There was

a smell of new paint and Jamaican cedar. The numbered
doors and the light fittings were in good taste. Bond's room
was almost at the end on the left. No. 20 was opposite. The
bell hop unlocked No. 24 and held the door for Bond. Air-
conditioned air gushed out. It was a pleasant modern double
bedroom and bath in grey and white. When he was alone,
Bond went to the air-conditioning control and turned it to
zero. Then he threw back the curtains and wound down the
two broad windows to let in real air. Outside, the sea whispered softly on an invisible beach and the moonlight
splashed the black shadows of palms across trim lawns. To
his left, where the yellow light of the entrance showed a corner of the gravel sweep, Bond heard his car being started up
and driven away, presumably to a parking lot which would,
he guessed, be at the rear so as not to spoil the impact of the
façade. He turned back into his room and inspected it
minutely. The only objects of suspicion were a large picture
on the wall above the two beds and the telephone. The picture was a Jamaican market scene painted locally. Bond
lifted it off its nail, but the wall behind was innocent. He
then took out a pocket knife, laid the telephone carefully, so
as not to shift the receiver, upside down on a bed, and very
quietly and carefully unscrewed the bottom plate. He smiled
his satisfaction. Behind the plate was a small microphone
joined by leads to the main cable inside the cradle. He
screwed back the plate with the same care and put the telephone quietly back on the night table. He knew the gadget. It
would be transistorized and of sufficient power to pick up a
conversation in normal tones anywhere in the room. It
crossed his mind to say very devout prayers out loud before
he went to bed. That would be a fitting prologue for the central recording device!

James Bond unpacked his few belongings and called Room Service. A Jamaican voice answered. Bond ordered a bottle of Walker's de Luxe Bourbon, three glasses, ice and, for nine o'clock, Eggs Benedict. The voice said, 'Sure, sir.' Bond then took off his clothes, put his gun and holster under a pillow, rang for the valet and had his suit taken away to be pressed. By the time he had taken a hot shower followed by an ice-cold one and pulled on a fresh pair of Sea Island cotton underpants the bourbon had arrived.

The best drink in the day is just before the first one (the Red Stripe didn't count). James Bond put ice in the glass and three fingers of the bourbon and swilled it round the glass to cool it and break it down with the ice. He pulled a chair up to the window, put a low table beside it, took *Profiles in Courage* by Jack Kennedy out of his suitcase, happened to open it at Edmund G. Ross ('I looked down into my open grave'), then went and sat down, letting the scented air, a compound of sea and trees, breathe over his body, naked save for the underpants. He drank the bourbon down in two long draughts and felt its friendly bite at the back of his throat and in his stomach. He filled up his glass again, this time with more ice to make it a weaker drink, and sat back and thought about Scaramanga.

What was the man doing now? Talking long distance with Havana or the States? Organizing things for tomorrow? It would be interesting to see these fat, frightened stockholders! If Bond knew anything, they would be a choice bunch of hoods, the type that had owned the Havana hotels and casinos in the old Batista days, the men that held the stock in Las Vegas, that looked after the action in Miami. And whose money was Scaramanga representing? There was so much hot money drifting around the Caribbean that it might be any

of the syndicates, any of the banana dictators from the islands or the mainland. And the man himself? It had been
damned fine shooting that had killed the two birds swerving
through the window of 3½. How in hell was Bond going to
take him? On an impulse, Bond went over to his bed and
took the Walther from under the pillow. He slipped out the
magazine and pumped the single round on to the counter-
pane. He tested the spring of the magazine and of the breech
and drew a quick bead on various objects round the room.
He found he was aiming an inch or so high. But that would
be because the gun was lighter without its loaded magazine.
He snapped the magazine back and tried again. Yes, that was
better. He pumped a round into the breech, put up the safety
and replaced the gun under the pillow. Then he went back
to his drink and picked up the book and forgot his worries in
the high endeavours of great men.

The eggs came and were good. The mousseline sauce
might have been mixed at Maxim's. Bond had the tray removed, poured himself a last drink and prepared for bed.
Scaramanga would certainly have a master key. Tomorrow,
Bond would whittle himself a wedge to jam the door. For
tonight, he upended his suitcase just inside the door and
balanced the three glasses on top of it. It was a simple booby
trap but it would give him all the warning he needed. Then
he took off his shorts and got into bed and slept.

A nightmare woke him, sweating, around two in the morning. He had been defending a fort. There were other defend-
ers with him, but they seemed to be wandering around
aimlessly, ineffectively, and when Bond shouted to rally
them they seemed not to hear him. Out on the plain, Scaramanga sat bassackwards on the café chair beside a huge
golden cannon. Every now and then, he put his long cigar to

the touch-hole and there came a tremendous flash of sound-
less flame. A black cannon ball, as big as a football, lobbed
up high in the air and crashed down into the fort with a shat-
tering noise of breaking timber. Bond was armed with nothing but a longbow, but even this he could not fire because,
every time he tried to fit the notch of the arrow into the gut,
the arrow slipped out of his fingers to the ground. He cursed
his clumsiness. Any moment now and a huge cannon ball
would land on the small open space where he was standing!
Out on the plain, Scaramanga reached his cigar to the touch-
hole. The black ball soared up. It was coming straight for
Bond! It landed just in front of him and came rolling very
slowly towards him, getting bigger and bigger, smoke and
sparks coming from its shortening fuse. Bond threw up an
arm to protect himself. Painfully, the arm crashed into the
side of the night table and Bond woke up.

Bond got out of bed, gave himself a cold shower and drank
a glass of water. By the time he was back in bed, he had forgotten the nightmare and he went quickly to sleep and slept
dreamlessly until 7.30 in the morning. He put on swimming
trunks, removed the barricade from in front of the door and
went out into the passage. To his left, a door into the garden
was open and sun streamed in. He went out and was walking over the dewy grass towards the beach when he heard a
curious thumping noise from among the palms on his right.
He walked over. It was Scaramanga, in trunks, attended by a
good-looking young Negro holding a flame-coloured Terry
cloth robe, doing exercises on a trampoline. Scaramanga's
body gleamed with sweat in the sunshine as he hurled himself high in the air from the stretched canvas and bounded
back, sometimes from his knees or his buttocks and sometimes even from his head.

It was an impressive exercise in gymnastics. The prominent third nipple over the heart made an obvious target! Bond walked thoughtfully down to the beautiful crescent of white sand fringed with gently clashing palm trees. He dived in and, because of the other man's example, swam twice as far as he had intended.

James Bond had a quick and small breakfast in his room, dressed, reluctantly because of the heat, in his dark suit, armed himself and went for a walk round the property. He quickly got the picture. The night, and the lighted façade, had covered up a half-project. The East Wing on the other side of the lobby was still lath and plaster. The body of the hotel—the restaurant, night club and living-rooms that were the tail of the T-shaped structure, were mock-ups—stages for a dress rehearsal hastily assembled with the essential props, carpets, light fixtures and a scattering of furniture, but stinking of fresh paint and wood shavings. Perhaps fifty men and women were at work, tacking up curtains, Hoovering carpets, fixing the electricity, but no one was employed on the essentials, the big cement mixers, the drills, the ironwork, that lay about behind the hotel like the abandoned toys of a giant. At a guess, the place would need another year and another five million dollars to become what the plans had said it was to be. Bond saw Scaramanga's problem. Someone was going to complain about this. Others would want to get out. But then again, others would want to buy in, but cheaply, and use it as a tax-loss to set against more profitable enterprises elsewhere. Better to have a capital asset, with the big tax concessions that Jamaica gave, than pay the money to Uncle Sam, Uncle Fidel, Uncle Trujillo, Uncle Leoni of Venezuela. So Scaramanga's job would be to blind his guests with pleasure, send them back half drunk to their syndicates. Would it work? Bond knew such people and he doubted it. They might go to bed drunk with a pretty coloured girl, but they would awake sober or they wouldn't have their jobs, they wouldn't be coming here with their discreet brief-cases.

He walked farther back on the property. He wanted to locate his car. He found it in a deserted lot behind the West Wing. The sun would get at where it was so he drove it forward and into the shade of a giant ficus tree. He checked the petrol and pocketed the ignition key. There were not too many small precautions he could take.

On the parking lot, the smell of the swamps was very strong. While it was still comparatively cool, he decided to walk farther. He soon came to the end of the young shrubs and guinea grass the landscaper had laid on. Behind these was desolation—a great area of sluggish streams and swampland from which the hotel land had been recovered. Egrets, shrikes and Louisiana herons rose and settled lazily, and there were strange insect noises and the call of frogs and gekkos. On what would probably be the border of the property a biggish stream meandered towards the sea, its muddy banks pitted with the holes of land crabs and water rats. As Bond approached there was a heavy splash and a man-sized alligator left the bank and showed its snout before submerging. Bond smiled to himself. No doubt, if the hotel got off the ground, all this area would be turned into an asset. There would be native boatmen, suitably attired as Arawak Indians, a landing-stage and comfortable boats, with fringed shades, from which the guests could view the 'tropical jungle' for an extra ten dollars on the bill.

Bond glanced at his watch. He strolled back. To the left, not yet screened by the young oleanders and crotons that

had been planted for this eventual purpose, were the
kitchens and laundry and staff quarters, the usual back quarters of a luxury hotel, and music, the heartbeat thump of Jamaican calypso, came from their direction—presumably the
Kingston combo rehearsing. Bond walked round and under
the portico into the main lobby. Scaramanga was at the desk
talking to the manager. When he heard Bond's footsteps on
the marble, he turned and looked and gave Bond a curt nod.
He was dressed as on the previous day, and the high white
cravat suited the elegance of the hall. He said 'Okay, then' to
the manager and, to Bond, 'Let's go take a look at the conference room.'

Bond followed him through the restaurant door and then
through another door to the right that opened into a lobby,
one of whose walls was taken up with the glasses and plates
of a buffet. Beyond this was another door. Scaramanga led
the way through into what would one day perhaps be a card
room or writing-room. Now there was nothing but a round
table in the centre of a wine-red carpet and seven white
leatherette arm-chairs with scratch pads and pencils in front
of them. The chair facing the door, presumably Scaramanga's, had a white telephone in front of it.

Bond went round the room and examined the windows
and the curtains and glanced at the wall brackets of the lighting. He said, 'The brackets could be bugged. And of course
there's the telephone. Like me to go over it?'

Scaramanga looked at Bond stonily. He said, 'No need to.
It's bugged all right. By me. Got to have a record of what's
said.'

Bond said, 'All right, then. Where do you want me to be?'

'Outside the door. Sitting reading a magazine or something. There'll be the general meeting this afternoon around

four. Tomorrow there'll mebbe be one or two smaller meetings, mebbe just me and one of the guys. I want all these
meetings not to be disturbed. Got it?'

'Seems simple enough. Now, isn't it about time you told
me the names of these men and more or less who they represent and which ones, if any, you're expecting trouble
from?'

Scaramanga said, 'Take a chair and a paper and pencil.' He
strolled up and down the room. 'First there's Mr Hendriks.
Dutchman. Represents the European money, mostly Swiss.
You needn't bother with him. He's not the arguing type.
Then there's Sam Binion from Detroit.'

'The Purple Gang?'

Scaramanga stopped in his stride and looked hard at
Bond. 'These are all respectable guys, Mister Whoosis.'

'Hazard is the name.'

'All right. Hazard, then. But respectable, you understand.
Don't go getting the notion that this is another Apalachian.
These are all solid business men. Get me? This Sam Binion,
for instance. He's in real estate. He and his friends are worth
mebbe twenty million bucks. See what I mean? Then there's
Leroy Gengerella. Miami. Owns Gengerella Enterprises. Big
shot in the entertainment world. He may cut up rough. Guys
in that line of business like quick profits and a quick
turnover. And Ruby Rotkopf, the hotel man from Vegas. He'll
ask the difficult questions because he'll already know most
of the answers from experience. Hal Garfinkel from Chicago.
He's in Labour Relations, like me. Represents a lot of Team-
ster Union funds. He shouldn't be any trouble. Those unions
have got so much money they don't know where to put it.
That makes five. Last comes Louie Paradise from Phoenix,
Arizona. Owns Paradise Slots, the biggest people in the one-

armed bandit business. Got casino interests too. I can't figure which way he'll bet. That's the lot.'

'And who do you represent, Mr Scaramanga?'

'Caribbean money.'

'Cuban?'

'I said Caribbean. Cuba's in the Caribbean, isn't it?'

'Castro or Batista?'

The frown was back. Scaramanga's right hand balled into a fist. 'I told you not to rile me, Mister. So don't go prying into my affairs or you'll get hurt. And that's for sure.' As if he could hardly control himself longer, the big man turned on his heel and strode brusquely out of the room.

James Bond smiled. He turned back to the list in front of him. A strong reek of high gangsterdom rose from the paper. But the name he was most interested in was Mr Hendriks who represented 'European money'. If that was his real name, and he was a Dutchman, so, James Bond reflected, was he.

He tore off three sheets of paper to efface the impression of his pencil and walked out and along into the lobby. A bulky man was approaching the desk from the entrance. He was sweating mightily in his unseasonable wooden-looking suit. He might have been anybody—an Antwerp diamond merchant, a German dentist, a Swiss bank manager. The pale, square-jowled face was totally anonymous. He put a heavy brief-case on the desk and said in a thick Central European accent, 'I am Mr Hendriks. I think it is that you have a room for me, isn't it?'

The cars began rolling up. Scaramanga was in evidence. He switched a careful smile of welcome on and off. No hands were shaken. The host was greeted either as 'Pistol' or 'Mr S' except by Mr Hendriks, who called him nothing.

Bond stood within earshot of the desk and fitted the names to the men. In general appearance they were all much of a muchness. Dark-faced, clean-shaven, around five feet six, hard-eyed above thinly smiling mouths, curt of speech to the manager. They all held firmly on to their brief-cases when the bell boys tried to add them to the luggage on the rubber-tyred barrows. They dispersed to their rooms along the East Wing. Bond took out his list and added hat-check notations to each one except Hendriks who was clearly etched in Bond's memory. Gengerella became 'Italian origin, mean, pursed mouth'; Rotkopf, 'Thick neck, totally bald, Jew'; Binion, 'Bat ears, scar down left cheek, limp'; Garfinkel, 'The toughest. Bad teeth, gun under right armpit'; and, finally, Paradise, 'Showman type, cocky, false smile, diamond ring'.

Scaramanga came up. 'What you writing?'

'Just notes to remember them by.'

'Gimme.' Scaramanga held out a demanding hand.

Bond gave him the list.

Scaramanga ran his eyes down it. He handed it back. 'Fair enough. But you needn't have mentioned the only gun you noticed. They'll all be protected. Except Hendriks, I guess. These kinda guys are nervous when they move abroad.'

'What of?'

Scaramanga shrugged. 'Mebbe the natives.'

'The last people who worried about the natives were the redcoats, perhaps a hundred and fifty years ago.'

'Who cares? See you in the bar around twelve. I'll be introducing you as my Personal Assistant.'

'That'll be fine.'

Scaramanga's brows came together. Bond strolled off in the direction of his bedroom. He proposed to needle this man, and go on needling until it came to a fight. For the time being the other man would probably take it because it seemed he needed Bond. But there would come a moment, probably on an occasion when there were witnesses, when his vanity would be so sharply pricked that he would draw. Then Bond would have a small edge, for it would be he who had thrown down the glove. The tactic was a crude one, but Bond could think of no other.

Bond verified that his room had been searched at some time during the morning—and by an expert. He always used a Hoffritz safety razor patterned on the old-fashioned heavy-toothed Gillette type. His American friend Felix Leiter had once bought him one in New York to prove that they were the best, and Bond had stayed with them. The handle of a safety razor is a reasonably sophisticated hideout for the minor tools of espionage—codes, microdot developers, cyanide and other pills. That morning Bond had set a minute nick on the screw base of the handle in line with the 'Z' of the maker's name engraved on the shaft. The nick was now a millimetre to the right of the 'Z'. None of his other little traps, handkerchiefs with indelible dots in particular places arranged in a certain order, the angle of his suitcase with the wall of the wardrobe, the semi-extracted lining of the breast pocket of his spare suit, the particular symmetry of certain dents in his tube of Maclean's toothpaste, had been bungled or disturbed. They all might have been by a meticulous servant, a trained valet. But Jamaican servants, for all their charm and willingness, are not of this calibre. No. Between nine and ten, when Bond was doing his rounds and was well away from the hotel, his room had received a thorough going-over by someone who knew his business.

Bond was pleased. It was good to know that the fight was well and truly joined. If he found a chance of making a foray into No. 20, he hoped that he would do better. He took a shower. Afterwards, as he brushed his hair, he looked at himself in the mirror with inquiry. He was feeling a hundred per cent fit, but he remembered the dull, lacklustre eyes that had looked back at him when he shaved after first entering The Park—the tense, preoccupied expression on his face. Now the grey-blue eyes looked back at him from the tanned face with the brilliant glint of suppressed excitement and accurate focus of the old days. He smiled ironically back at the introspective scrutiny that so many people make of themselves before a race, a contest of wits, a trial of some sort. He had no excuses. He was ready to go.

The bar was through a brass-studded leather door opposite the lobby to the conference room. It was—in the fashion—a mock-English public-house saloon bar with luxury accessories. The scrubbed wooden chairs and benches had foam-rubber squabs in red leather. Behind the bar, the tankards were of silver, or simulated silver, instead of pewter. The hunting prints, copper and brass hunting horns, muskets and powder horns, on the walls could have come from the Parker Galleries in London. Instead of tankards of beer, bottles of champagne in antique coolers stood on the tables and, instead of yokels, the hoods stood around in what looked like Brooks Brothers 'tropical' attire and carefully sipped their drinks while 'Mine Host' leant against the polished mahogany bar and twirled his golden gun round and round on the first finger of his right hand like the snide poker cheat out of an old Western.

As the door closed behind Bond with a pressurized sigh, the golden gun halted in mid-whirl and sighted on Bond's stomach. 'Fellers,' said Scaramanga, mock boisterous, 'meet my Personal Assistant, Mr Mark Hazard, from London, England. He's come along to make things run smoothly over this week-end. Mark, come over and meet the gang and pass round the canapés.' He lowered the gun and shoved it into his waistband.

James Bond stitched a Personal Assistant smile on his face and walked up to the bar. Perhaps because he was an Englishman, there was a round of handshaking. The red-coated barman asked him what he would have and he said, 'Some pink gin. Plenty of bitters. Beefeater's.' There was desultory talk about the relative merits of gins. Everyone else seemed to be drinking champagne except Mr Hendriks who stood away from the group and nursed a Schweppes Bitter Lemon. Bond moved among the men. He made small talk about their flight, the weather in the States, the beauties of Jamaica. He wanted to fit the voices to the names. He gravitated towards Mr Hendriks. 'Seems we're the only two Europeans here. Gather you're from Holland. Often passed through. Never stayed there long. Beautiful country.'

The very pale blue eyes regarded Bond unenthusiastically. 'Sank you.'

'What part do you come from?'

'Den Haag.'

'Have you lived there long?'

'Many, many years.'

'Beautiful town.'

'Sank you.'

'Is this your first visit to Jamaica?'

'No.'

'How do you like it?'

'It is a beautiful place.'

Bond nearly said, 'Sank you.' He smiled encouragingly at Mr Hendriks as much as to say, 'I've made all the running so far. Now you say something.'

Mr Hendriks looked past Bond's right ear at nothing. The pressure of the silence built up. Mr Hendriks shifted his weight from one foot to the other and finally broke down. His eyes shifted and looked thoughtfully at Bond. 'And you. You are from London, isn't it?'

'Yes. Do you know it?'

'I have been there, yes.'

'Where do you usually stay?'

There was hesitation. 'With friends.'

'That must be convenient.'

'Pliss?'

'I mean it's pleasant to have friends in a foreign town. Hotels are so much alike.'

'I have not found this. Excuse pliss.' With a Germanic bob of the head Mr Hendriks moved decisively away from Bond

and went up to Scaramanga, who was still lounging in solitary splendour at the bar. Mr Hendriks said something. His
words acted like a command on the other man. Mr Scaramanga straightened himself and followed Mr Hendriks into
a far corner of the room. He stood and listened with deference as Mr Hendriks talked rapidly in a low tone.

Bond, joining the other men, was interested. It was his
guess that no other man in the room could have buttonholed
Scaramanga with so much authority. He noticed that many
fleeting glances were cast in the direction of the couple
apart. For Bond's money, this was either the Mafia or KGB.
Probably even the other five wouldn't know which, but they
would certainly recognize the secret smell of 'The Machine'
which Mr Hendriks exuded so strongly.

Luncheon was announced. The Jamaican head waiter hov-
ered between two richly prepared tables. There were place
cards. Bond found that, while Scaramanga was host at one of
them, he himself was at the head of the other table between
Mr Paradise and Mr Rotkopf. As he expected, Mr Paradise
was the better value of the two and, as they went through the
conventional shrimp cocktail, steak, fruit salad of the Amer-
icanized hotel abroad, Bond cheerfully got himself involved
in an argument about the odds at roulette when there are one
zero or two. Mr Rotkopf's only contribution was to say,
through a mouthful of steak and French fried, that he had
once tried three zeros at the Black Cat Casino in Miami but
that the experiment had failed. Mr Paradise said that so it
should have. 'You got to let the suckers win sometimes,
Ruby, or they won't come back. Sure, you can squeeze the
juice out of them, but you oughta leave them the pips. Like
with my slots. I tell the customers, don't be too greedy. Don't
set 'em at thirty per cent for the house. Set 'em at twenty. You

ever heard of Mr J. B. Morgan turning down a net profit of twenty per cent? Hell, no! So why try and be smarter than guys like that?'

Mr Rotkopf said sourly, 'You got to make big profits to put against a bum steer like this.' He waved a hand. 'If you ask me,' he held up a bit of steak on his fork, 'you're eating the only money you're going to see out of this dump at this minute.'

Mr Paradise leaned across the table and said softly, 'You know something?'

Mr Rotkopf said, 'I always told my money that the bindweed would get this place. The dam' fools wouldn't listen. And look where we are in three years! Second mortgage nearly run out and we've only got one storey up. What I say is . . .'

The argument went off into the realms of high finance. At the next-door table there was not even this amount of animation. Scaramanga was a man of few words. There were clearly none available for social occasions. Opposite him, Mr Hendriks exuded a silence as thick as Gouda cheese. The three hoods addressed an occasional glum sentence to anyone who would listen. James Bond wondered how Scaramanga was going to electrify this unpromising company into 'having a good time'.

Luncheon broke up and the company dispersed to their rooms. James Bond wandered round to the back of the hotel and found a discarded shingle on a rubbish dump. It was blazing hot under the afternoon sun, but the Doctor's wind was blowing in from the sea. For all its air-conditioning, there was something grim about the impersonal grey and white of Bond's bedroom. Bond walked along the shore, took off his coat and tie and sat in the shade of a bush of sea grapes and watched the fiddler crabs about their minuscule business in the sand while he whittled two chunky wedges out of the Jamaican cedar. Then he closed his eyes and thought about Mary Goodnight. She would now be having her siesta in some villa on the outskirts of Kingston. It would probably be high up in the Blue Mountains for the coolness. In Bond's imagination, she would be lying on her bed under a mosquito net. Because of the heat, she would have nothing on, and one could see only an ivory and gold shape through the fabric of the net. But one would know that there were small beads of sweat on her upper lip and between her breasts and the fringes of the golden hair would be damp. Bond took off his clothes and lifted up the corner of the mosquito net, not wanting to wake her until he had fitted himself against her thighs. But she turned, in half sleep, towards him and held out her arms. 'James . . .'

Under the sea-grape bush, a hundred and twenty miles away from the scene of the dream, James Bond's head came up with a jerk. He looked quickly, guiltily, at his watch. 3.30. He went off to his room and had a cold shower, verified that his cedar wedges would do what they were meant to do, and strolled down the corridor to the lobby.

The manager with the neat suit and neat face came out from behind his desk. 'Er, Mr Hazard.'

'Yes.'

'I don't think you've met my assistant, Mr Travis.'

'No, I don't think I have.'

'Would you care to step into the office for a moment and shake him by the hand?'

'Later perhaps. We've got this conference on in a few minutes.'

The neat man came a step closer. He said quietly, 'He particularly wants to meet you, Mr—er—Bond.'

Bond cursed himself. This was always happening in his particular trade. You were looking in the dark for a beetle with red wings. Your eyes were focused for that particular pattern on the bark of the tree. You didn't notice the moth with cryptic colouring that crouched quietly near by, itself like a piece of the bark, itself just as important to the collector. The focus of your eyes was too narrow. Your mind was too concentrated. You were using 1 x 100 magnification and your 1 x 10 was not in focus. Bond looked at the man with the recognition that exists between crooks, between homosexuals, between secret agents. It is the look common to men bound by secrecy—by common trouble. 'Better make it quick.'

The neat man stepped behind his desk and opened a door. Bond went in and the neat man closed the door behind them. A tall, slim man was standing at a filing cabinet. He turned. He had a lean, bronzed Texan face under an unruly mop of straight, fair hair, and, instead of a right hand, a bright steel hook. Bond stopped in his tracks. His face split into a smile broader than he had smiled for what? Was it three years or four? He said, 'You goddamned, lousy crook. What in hell are you doing here?' He went up to the man and hit him hard on the biceps of the left arm.

The grin was slightly more creased than Bond remembered, but it was just as friendly and ironical. Mr Travis said, 'The name is Leiter, Mr Felix Leiter. Temporary accountant on loan from Morgan Guarantee Trust to the Thunderbird Hotel. We're just checking up on your credit rating, Mr Hazard. Would you kindly, in your royal parlance, extract your finger, and give me some evidence that you are who you claim to be?'

James Bond, almost light-headed with pleasure, picked up a handful of travel literature from the front desk, said 'Hi!' to Mr Gengerella, who didn't reply, and followed him into the conference room lobby. They were the last to show. Scaramanga, beside the open door to the conference room, looked pointedly at his watch and said to Bond, 'Okay, feller. Lock the door when we're all settled and don't let anyone in even if the hotel catches fire.' He turned to the barman behind the loaded buffet. 'Get lost, Joe. I'll call for you later.' He said to the room, 'Right. We're all set. Let's go.' He led the way into the conference room and the six men followed. Bond stood by the door and noted the seating order round the table. He closed the door and locked it and quickly also locked the exit from the lobby. Then he picked up a champagne glass from the buffet, pulled over a chair and sited the chair very close to the door of the conference room. He placed the bowl of the champagne glass as near as possible to a hinge of the door and, holding the glass by the stem, put his left ear up against its base. Through the crude amplifier, what had been the rumble of a voice became Mr Hendriks speaking, '. . . and so it is that I will now report from my superiors in Europe . . .' The voice paused and Bond heard another noise, the creak of a chair. Like lightning he pulled the chair back a few feet, opened one of the travel folders on his lap and raised the glass to his lips. The door jerked open and Scaramanga stood in the opening, twirling his pass key on a chain. He examined the innocent figure on the chair. He said, 'Okay, feller. Just checking,' and kicked the door shut. Bond noisily locked it and took up his place again. Mr Hendriks said, 'I have one most important message for our Chairman. It is from a sure source. There is a man that is called James Bond that is looking for him in this territory. This is a man who is from the British Secret Service. I have no informations or descriptions of this man but it seems that he is highly rated by my superiors. Mr Scaramanga, have you heard of this man?'

Scaramanga snorted. 'Hell, no! And should I care? I eat one of their famous secret agents for breakfast from time to time. Only ten days ago, I disposed of one of them who came nosing after me. Man called Ross. His body is now very slowly sinking to the bottom of a pitch lake in Eastern Trinidad—place called La Brea. The oil company, the Trinidad Lake Asphalt people will obtain an interesting barrel of crude one of these days. Next question, please, Mr Hendriks.'

'Next I am wishing to know what is the policy of The Group in the matter of cane sabotage. At our meeting six months ago in Havana, against my minority vote, it was decided, in exchange for certain favours, to come to the aid of Fidel Castro and assist in maintaining and indeed increasing the world price of sugar to offset the damage caused by Hurricane Flora. Since this time there have been very numerous

fires in the cane fields of Jamaica and Trinidad. In this connection, it has come to the ears of my superiors that individual members of The Group, notably,' there was the rustle of
paper, 'Messrs Gengerella, Rotkopf and Binion, in addition
to our Chairman, have engaged in extensive purchasing of
July sugar futures for the benefit of private gain . . .'

There came an angry murmur from round the table. 'Why
shouldn't we . . .? Why shouldn't they . . .?' The voice of
Gengerella dominated the others. He shouted, 'Who in hell
said we weren't to make money? Isn't that one of the objects
of The Group? I ask you again, Mr Hendriks, as I asked you
six months ago, who in hell is it among your so-called "superiors" who wants to keep the price of raw sugar down?
For my money, the most interested party in such a gambit
would be Soviet Russia. They're selling goods to Cuba, including, let me say, the recently abortive shipment of mis-
siles to fire against my homeland, in exchange for raw sugar.
They're sharp traders, the Reds. In their double-dealing
way, even from a friend and ally, they would want more
sugar for fewer goods. Yes? I suppose,' the voice sneered,
'one of your superiors, Mr Hendriks, would not by any
chance be in the Kremlin?'

The voice of Scaramanga cut through the ensuing hubbub.
'Fellers! Fellers!' A reluctant silence fell. 'When we formed
the Co-operative, it was agreed that the first object was to co-
operate with one another. Okay, then. Mr Hendriks. Let me
put you more fully in the picture. So far as the total finances
of The Group are concerned, we have a fine situation coming up. As an investment group, we have good bets and bad
bets. Sugar is a good bet and we should ride that bet even
though certain members of The Group have chosen not to be
on the horse. Get me? Now hear me through. There are six

ships controlled by The Group at this moment riding at anchor outside New York and other US harbours. These ships are loaded with raw sugar. These ships, Mr Hendriks, will not dock and unload until sugar futures, July futures, have risen another ten cents. In Washington, the Department of Agriculture and the Sugar Lobby know this. They know that we have them by the balls. Meantimes the Liquor Lobby is leaning on them—let alone Russia. The price of molasses is going up with sugar and the rum barons are kicking up hell and want our ships let in before there's a real shortage and the price goes through the roof. But there's another side to it. We're having to pay our crews and our charter bills and so on, and squatting ships are dead ships, dead losses. So something's going to give. In the business, the situation we've developed is called the Floating Crop Game—our ships lying offshore, lined up against the Government of the United States. All right. So now four of us stand to win or lose ten million bucks or so—us and our backers. And we've got this little business of the Thunderbird on the red side of the sheet. So what do you think, Mr Hendriks? Of course we burn the crops where we can get away with it. I got a good man in with the Rastafaris—that's a beat sect here that grows beards and smokes ganja and mostly lives on a bit of land outside Kingston called the Dungle—the Dunghill—and believes it owes allegiance to the King of Ethiopia, this King Zog or what-have-you, and that that's their rightful home. So I've got a man in there, a man who wants the ganja for them, and I keep him supplied in exchange for plenty fires and troubles on the cane lands. So all right, Mr Hendriks. You just tell your superiors that what goes up must come down and that applies to the price of sugar like anything else. Okay?'

Mr Hendriks said, 'I will pass on your saying, Mr Scaramanga. It will not cause pleasure. Now there is this business
of the hotel. How is she standing, if you pliss? I think we are
all wishing to know the true situation, isn't it?'

There was a growl of assent.

Mr Scaramanga went off into a long dissertation which
was only of passing interest to Bond. Felix Leiter would in
any case be getting it all on the tape in a drawer of his filing
cabinet. He had reassured Bond on this score. The neat
American, Leiter had explained, filling him in with the essentials, was in fact a certain Mr Nick Nicholson of the CIA.
His particular concern was Mr Hendriks who, as Bond had
suspected, was a top man of the KGB. The KGB favours
oblique control—a man in Geneva being the Resident Director for Italy, for instance—and Mr Hendriks at The Hague
was in fact Resident Director for the Caribbean and in charge
of the Havana centre. Leiter was still working for Pinkertons,
but was also on the reserve of the CIA who had drafted him
for this particular assignment because of his knowledge,
gained in the past mostly with James Bond, of Jamaica. His
job was to get a breakdown of The Group and find out what
they were up to. They were all well-known hoods who
would normally have been the concern of the FBI, but Gengerella was a Capo Mafiosi and this was the first time the
Mafia had been found consorting with the KGB—a most dis-
turbing partnership which must at all costs be quickly broken up, by physical elimination if need be. Nick Nicholson,
whose 'front' name was Mr Stanley Jones, was an electronics
expert. He had traced the main lead to Scaramanga's recording device under the floor of the central switch room and
had bled off the microphone cable to his own tape recorder
in the filing cabinet. So Bond had not much to worry about.

He was listening to satisfy his own curiosity and to fill in on anything that might transpire in the lobby or out of range of the bug in the telephone on the conference room table. Bond had explained his own presence. Leiter had given a long low whistle of respectful apprehension. Bond had agreed to keep well clear of the other two men and to paddle his own canoe, but they had arranged an emergency meeting place and a postal 'drop' in the uncompleted and 'Out of Order' men's room off the lobby. Nicholson had given him a pass key for this place and all other rooms and then Bond had had to hurry off to his meeting. James Bond was immensely reassured by finding these unexpected reinforcements. He had worked with Leiter on some of his most hazardous assignments. There was no man like him when the chips were down. Although Leiter had only a steel hook instead of a right arm—a memento of one of those assignments—he was one of the finest left-handed one-armed shots in the States and the hook itself could be a devastating weapon at close quarters.

Scaramanga was finishing his exposition. 'So the net of it is, gentlemen, that we need to find ten million bucks. The interests I represent, which are the majority interests, suggest that this sum should be provided by a Note issue, bearing interest at ten per cent and repayable in ten years, such an issue to have priority over all other loans.'

The voice of Mr Rotkopf broke in angrily. 'The hell it will! Not on your life, Mister. What about the seven per cent second mortgage put up by me and my friends only a year back? What do you think I'd get if I went back to Vegas with that kind of parley? The old heave-ho! And at that I'm being optimistic.'

'Beggars can't be choosers, Ruby. It's that or close. What do you other fellers have to say?'

Hendriks said, 'Ten per cent on a first charge is good pizzness. My friends and I will take one million dollars. On the understanding, it is natural, that the conditions of the issue are, how shall I say, more substantial, less open to misunderstandings, than the second mortgage of Mr Rotkopf and his friends.'

'Of course. And I and my friends will also take a million. Sam?'

Mr Binion said reluctantly, 'Okay, okay. Count us in for the same. But by golly this has got to be the last touch.'

'Mr Gengerella?'

'It sounds a good bet. I'll take the rest.'

The voices of Mr Garfinkel and Mr Paradise broke in excitedly, Garfinkel in the lead. 'Like hell you will! I'm taking a million.'

'And so am I,' shouted Mr Paradise. 'Cut the cake equally. But dammit. Let's be fair to Ruby. Ruby, you oughta have first pick. How much do you want? You can have it off the top.'

'I don't want a damned cent of your phoney Notes. As soon as I get back, I'm going to reach for the best damned lawyers in the States—all of them. You think you can scrub a mortgage just by saying so, you've all got another think coming.'

There was silence. The voice of Scaramanga was soft and deadly. 'You're making a big mistake, Ruby. You've just got yourself a nice fat tax-loss to put against your Vegas interests. And don't forget that when we formed this Group we all took an oath. None of us was to operate against the interests of the others. Is that your last word?'

'It dam' is.'

'Would this help you change your mind? They've got a slogan for it in Cuba—*Rapido! Seguro! Economico!* This is how the system operates.'

The scream of terror and the explosion were simultaneous. A chair crashed to the floor and there was a moment's silence. Then someone coughed nervously. Mr Gengerella said calmly, 'I think that was the correct solution of an embarrassing conflict of interests. Ruby's friends in Vegas like a quiet life. I doubt if they will even complain. It is better to be a live owner of some finely engraved paper than to be a dead holder of a second mortgage. Put them in for a million, Pistol. I think you behaved with speed and correctness. Now then, can you clean this up?'

'Sure, sure.' Mr Scaramanga's voice was relaxed, happy. 'Ruby's left here to go back to Vegas. Never heard of again. We don't know nuthen'. I've got some hungry crocs out back there in the river. They'll give him free transportation to where he's going—and his baggage if it's good leather. I shall need some help tonight. What about you, Sam? And you, Louie?'

The voice of Mr Paradise pleaded. 'Count me out, Pistol. I'm a good Catholic.'

Mr Hendriks said, 'I will take his place. I am not a Catholic person.'

'So be it then. Well, fellers, any other business? If not, we'll break up the meeting and have a drink.'

Hal Garfinkel said nervously, 'Just a minute, Pistol. What about that guy outside the door? That limey feller? What's he going to say about the fireworks and all?'

Mr Scaramanga's chuckle was like the dry chuckle of a gekko. 'Just don't you worry your tiny head about the limey, Hal. He'll be looked after when the week-end's over. Picked him up in a bordello in a village near by. Place where I go get my weed and a bit of black tail. Got only temporary staff here to see you fellers have a good time over the week-end. He's the temporariest of the lot. Those crocs have a big appetite. Ruby'll be the main dish, but they'll need a dessert. Jes' you leave him to me. For all I know he may be this James Bond man Mr Hendriks has told us about. I should worry. I don't like limeys. Like some good yankee once said, "For every Britisher that dies, there's a song in my heart." Remember the guy? Around the time of the Israeli war against them. I dig that viewpoint. Stuck-up bastards. Stuffed shirts. When the time comes, I'm going to let the stuffing out of this one. Jes' you leave him to me. Or let's jes' say leave him to this.'

Bond smiled a thin smile. He could imagine the golden gun being produced and twirled round the finger and stuck back in the waistband. He got up and moved his chair away from the door and poured champagne into the useful glass and leant against the buffet and studied the latest hand-out from the Jamaica Tourist Board.

The click of Scaramanga's pass key sounded in the lock. Scaramanga looked at Bond from the doorway. He ran a finger along the small moustache. 'Okay, feller. I guess that's enough of the house champagne. Cut along to the manager and tell him Mr Ruby Rotkopf'll be checking out tonight. I'll fix the details. And say a major fuse blew during the meeting and I'm going to seal off this room and find out why we're having so much bad workmanship around the place. 'Kay? Then drinks and dinner and bring on the dancing girls. Got the photo?'

James Bond said that he had. He weaved slightly as he went to the lobby door and unlocked it. 'E & OE—Errors and omissions excepted' as the financial prospectuses say, he thought that he had indeed now 'got the photo'. And it was an exceptionally clear print in black and white without 'fuzz'.

In the back office, James Bond went quickly over the highlights of the meeting. Nick Nicholson and Felix Leiter agreed they had enough on the tape, supported by Bond, to send Scaramanga to the chair. That night, one of them would do some snooping while the body of Rotkopf was being disposed of and try and get enough evidence to have Garfinkel and, better still, Hendriks indicted as accessories. But they didn't at all like the outlook for James Bond. Felix commanded him, 'Now don't you move an inch without that old equalizer of yours. We don't want to have to read that obituary of yours in *The Times* all over again. All that crap about what a splendid feller you are nearly made me throw up when I saw it reprinted in the American blatts. I dam' nearly fired off a piece to the *Trib* putting the record straight.'

Bond laughed. He said, 'You're a fine friend, Felix. When I think of all the trouble I've been to to set you a good example all these years.' He went off to his room, swallowed two heavy slugs of bourbon, had a cold shower and lay on his bed and looked at the ceiling until it was 8.30 and time for dinner. The meal was less stuffy than luncheon. Everyone seemed satisfied with the way the business of the day had gone and all except Scaramanga and Mr Hendriks had obviously had plenty to drink. Bond found himself excluded from the happy talk. Eyes avoided his and replies to his attempts at conversation were monosyllabic. He was bad news. He had been dealt the death card by the boss. He was certainly not a man to be pally with. While the meal moved sluggishly on—the conventional 'expensive' dinner of a cruise ship, desiccated smoked salmon with a thimbleful of small-grained black caviar, fillets of some unnamed native fish, possibly silk fish, in a cream sauce, 'poulet suprême', a badly roasted broiler with a thick gravy, and *bombe surprise*, was as predictable as such things are—the dining-room was being turned into a 'tropical jungle' with the help of potted plants, piles of oranges and coconuts and an occasional stem of bananas, as a backdrop for the calypso band which, in wine-red and gold frilled shirts, in due course assembled and began playing 'Linstead Market' too loud. The tune closed. An acceptable but heavily clad girl appeared and began singing 'Belly-Lick' with the printable words. She wore a false pineapple as a head-dress. Bond saw a 'cruise ship' evening stretching ahead. He decided that he was either too old or too young for the worst torture of all, boredom, and got up and went to the head of the table. He said to Mr Scaramanga, 'I've got a headache. I'm going to bed.'

Mr Scaramanga looked up at him under lizard eyelids. 'No. If you figure the evening's not going so good, make it go better. That's what you're being paid for. You act as if you know Jamaica. Okay. Get these people off the pad.'

It was many years since James Bond had accepted a 'dare'. He felt the eyes of The Group on him. What he had drunk had made him careless—perhaps wanting to show off, like the man at the party who insists on playing the drums. Stupidly, he wanted to assert his personality over this bunch of tough guys who rated him insignificant. He didn't stop to think that it was bad tactics, that he would be better off being the ineffectual limey. He said, 'All right, Mr Scaramanga. Give me a hundred-dollar bill and your gun.'

Scaramanga didn't move. He looked up at Bond with surprise and controlled uncertainty. Louie Paradise shouted thickly, 'C'mon, Pistol! Let's see some action! Mebbe the guy can produce.'

Scaramanga reached for his hip pocket, took out his billfold and thumbed out a note. Next he slowly reached to his waistband and took out his gun. The subdued light from the spot on the girl glowed on its gold. He laid the two objects on the table side by side. James Bond, his back to the cabaret, picked up the gun and hefted it. He thumbed back the hammer and twirled the cylinder with a flash of his hands to verify that it was loaded. Then he suddenly whirled, dropped on his knee so that his aim would be above the shadowy musicians in the background and, his arm at full length, let fly. The explosion was deafening in the confined space. The music died. There was a tense silence. The remains of the false pineapple hit something in the dark background with a soft thud. The girl stood under the spot and put her hands to her face and slowly folded to the dance floor like something graceful out of *Swan Lake*. The maître d'hôtel came running from among the shadows.

As chatter broke out among The Group, James Bond picked up the hundred-dollar note and walked out into the spotlight. He bent down and lifted the girl up by her arm. He pushed the dollar bill down into her cleavage. He said, 'That was a fine act we did together, sweetheart. Don't worry. You were in no danger. I aimed for the top half of the pineapple. Now run off and get ready for your next turn.' He turned her round and gave her a sharp pat on the behind. She gave him a horrified glance and scurried off into the shadows.

Bond strolled on and came up with the band. 'Who's in charge here? Who's in command of the show?'

The guitarist, a tall, gaunt Negro, got slowly to his feet. The whites of his eyes showed. He squinted at the golden gun in Bond's hand. He said uncertainly, as if signing his own death warrant, 'Me, sah.'

'What's your name?'

'King Tiger, sah.'

'All right then, King. Now listen to me. This isn't a Salvation Army fork-supper. Mr Scaramanga's friends want some action. And they want it hot. I'll be sending plenty of rum over to loosen things up. Smoke weed if you like. We're private here. No one's going to tell on you. And get that pretty girl back, but with only half the clothes on, and tell her to come up close and sing "Belly-Lick" very clearly with the blue words. And, by the end of the show, she and the other girls have got to end up stripped. Understand? Now get cracking or the evening'll fold and there'll be no tips at the end. Okay? Then let's go.'

There was nervous laughter and whispered exhortation to King Tiger from the six-piece combo. King Tiger grinned broadly. 'Okay, Captain, sah.' He turned to his men. 'Give 'em "Iron Bar", but hot. An' I'll go get some steam up with Daisy and her friends.' He strode to the service exit and the band crashed into its stride.

Bond walked back and laid the pistol down in front of Scaramanga, who gave Bond a long, inquisitive look and slid it back into his waistband. He said flatly, 'We must have a shooting match one of these days, Mister. How about it? Twenty paces and no wounding?'

'Thanks,' said Bond, 'but my mother wouldn't approve. Would you have some rum sent over to the band? These people can't play dry.' He went back to his seat. He was hardly noticed. The five men, or rather four of them because Hendriks sat impassively through the whole evening, were straining their ears to catch the lewd words of the Fanny Hill version of 'Iron Bar' that were coming across clearly from the soloist. Four girls, plump, busty little animals wearing nothing but white sequined G-strings, ran out on to the floor, and, advancing towards the audience, did an enthusiastic belly dance that brought sweat to the temples of Louie Paradise and Hal Garfinkel. The number ended amidst applause, the girls ran off and the lights were dowsed, leaving only the circular spot in the middle of the floor. The drummer, on his calypso box, began a hasty beat like a quickened pulse. The service door opened and shut and a curious object was wheeled into the circle of light. It was a huge hand, perhaps six feet tall at its highest point, upholstered in black leather. It stood, half open on its broad base, with the thumb and fingers outstretched as if ready to catch something. The drummer hastened his beat. The service door sighed. A glistening figure slipped through and, after pausing in the darkness, moved into the pool of light round the hand with a strutting jerk of belly and limbs. There was Chinese blood in her and her body, totally naked and shining with palm oil, was almost white against the black hand. As she jerked round the hand she caressed its outstretched fingers with her hands and arms and then, with well-acted swooning motions, climbed into the palm of the hand and proceeded to perform langorous, but explicit and ingenious acts of passion with each of the fingers in turn. The scene, the black hand, now shining with her oil and seeming to clutch at the squirming white body, was of an incredible lewdness, and Bond, himself aroused, noticed that even Scaramanga was watching with rapt attention, his eyes narrow slits. The drummer had now worked up to his crescendo. The girl, in well-simulated ecstasy, mounted the thumb, slowly expired upon it and then, with a last grind of her rump, slid down it and vanished through the exit. The act was over. The lights came on and everyone, including the band, applauded loudly. The men came out of their separate animal trances. Scaramanga clapped his hand for the band leader, took a note out of his case and said something to him under his breath. The chieftain, Bond suspected, had chosen his bride for the night!

After this inspired piece of sexual dumb crambo, the rest of the cabaret was an anti-climax. One of the girls, only after her G-string had been slashed off with a cutlass by the band leader, was able to squirm under a bamboo balanced just eighteen inches off the floor on the top of two beer bottles. The first girl, the one who had acted as an unwitting pineapple-tree to Bond's William Tell act, came on and combined an acceptable strip-tease with a rendering of 'Belly-Lick' that got the audience straining its ears again, and then the whole team of six girls, less the Chinese beauty, came up to the audience and invited them to dance. Scaramanga and Hendriks refused with adequate politeness and Bond stood the two left-out girls glasses of champagne and learned that their names were Mabel and Pearl while he watched the four others being almost bent in half by the bear-like embraces of the four sweating hoods as they clumsily cha-cha'd round the room to the now riotous music of the half-drunk band. The climax to what could certainly class as an orgy was clearly in sight. Bond told his two girls that he must go to the men's room and slipped away when Scaramanga was looking elsewhere, but, as he went, he noted that Hendrik's gaze, as cool as if he had been watching an indifferent film, was firmly on him as he made his escape.

When Bond got to his room, it was midnight. His windows had been closed and the air conditioning turned on. He switched it off and opened the windows half-way and then, with heartfelt relief, took a shower and went to bed. He worried for a while about having shown off with the gun, but it was an act of folly which he couldn't undo and he soon went to sleep to dream of three black-cloaked men dragging a shapeless bundle through dappled moonlight towards dark waters that were dotted with glinting red eyes. The gnashing white teeth and the crackling bones resolved themselves into a persistent scrabbling noise that brought him suddenly awake. He looked at the luminous dial of his watch. It said 3.30. The scrabbling became a quiet tapping from behind the curtains. James Bond slid quietly out of bed, took his gun from under his pillow and crept softly along the wall to the edge of the curtains. He pulled them aside with one swift motion. The golden hair shone almost silver in the moonlight. Mary Goodnight whispered urgently, 'Quick, James! Help me in!'

Bond cursed softly to himself. What the hell? He laid his gun down on the carpet and reached for her outstretched hands and half dragged, half pulled her over the sill. At the last moment, her heel caught in the frame and the window banged shut with a noise like a pistol shot. Bond cursed again, softly and fluently, under his breath. Mary Goodnight whispered penitently, 'I'm terribly sorry, James.'

Bond shushed her. He picked up his gun and put it back

under his pillow and led her across the room and into the bathroom. He turned on the light and, as a precaution, the shower, and, simultaneously with her gasp, remembered he was naked. He said, 'Sorry, Goodnight,' and reached for a towel and wound it round his waist and sat down on the edge of the bath. He gestured to the girl to sit down on the lavatory seat and said, with icy control, 'What in hell are you doing here, Mary?'

Her voice was desperate. 'I had to come. I had to find you somehow. I got on to you through the girl at that, er, dreadful place. I left the car in the trees down the drive and just sniffed about. There were lights on in some of the rooms and I listened and, er,' she blushed crimson, 'I gathered you couldn't be in any of them and then I saw the open window and I just somehow knew you would be the only one to sleep with his window open. So I just had to take the chance.'

'Well, we've got to get you out of here as quick as we can. Anyway, what's the trouble?'

'A "Most Immediate" in Triple-X came over this evening. I mean yesterday evening. It was to be passed to you at all costs. HQ thinks you're in Havana. It said that one of the KGB top men who goes under the name of Hendriks is in the area and that he's known to be visiting this hotel. You're to keep away from him. They know from "a delicate but sure source"' (Bond smiled at the old euphemism for cypher-breaking) 'that among his other jobs is to find you and, er, well, kill you. So I put two and two together, and, what with you being in this corner of the island and the questions you asked me, I guessed that you might be already on his track but that you might be walking into an ambush, sort of. Not knowing, I mean, that while you were after him, he was after you.'

She put out a tentative hand, as if for reassurance that she had done the right thing. Bond took it and patted it absentmindedly while his mind chewed on this new complication. He said, 'The man's here all right. So's a gunman called Scaramanga. You might as well know, Mary, that Scaramanga killed Ross. In Trinidad.' She put her hand up to her mouth. 'You can report it as a fact, from me. If I can get you out of here, that is. As for Hendriks, he's here all right, but he doesn't seem to have identified me for certain. Did HQ say whether he was given a description of me?'

'You were simply described as "the notorious secret agent, James Bond". But this doesn't seem to have meant much to Hendriks because he asked for particulars. That was two days ago. He may get them cabled or telephoned here at any minute. You do see why I had to come, James?'

'Yes, of course. And thanks, Mary. Now, I've got to get you out of that window and then you must just make your own way. Don't worry about me. I think I can handle the situation all right. Besides, I've got help.' He told her about Felix Leiter and Nicholson. 'You just tell HQ you've delivered the message and that I'm here and about the two CIA men. HQ can get the CIA angles from Washington direct. Okay?' He got to his feet.

She stood up beside him and looked up at him. 'But you will take care?'

'Sure, sure.' He patted her shoulder. He turned off the shower and opened the bathroom door. 'Now, come on. We must pray for a stroke of luck.'

A silken voice from the darkness at the end of the bed said, 'Well, the Holy Man jes' ain't running for you today, Mister. Step forward both of you. Hands clasped behind the neck.'

Scaramanga walked to the door and turned the lights on. He was naked save for his shorts and the holster below his left arm. The golden gun remained trained on Bond as he moved.

Bond looked at him incredulously, then to the carpet inside the door. The wedges were still there, undisturbed. He could not possibly have got through the window unaided. Then he saw that his clothes cupboard stood open and that light showed through into the next room. It was the simplest of secret doors—just the whole of the back of the cupboard, impossible to detect from Bond's side of the wall and, on the other, probably, in appearance, a locked communicating door.

Scaramanga came back into the centre of the room and stood looking at them both. His mouth and eyes sneered. He said, 'I didn't see this piece of tail in the line-up. Where you been keeping it, buster? And why d'you have to hide it away in the bathroom? Like doing it under the shower?'

Bond said, 'We're engaged to be married. She works in the British High Commissioner's Office in Kingston. Cypher clerk. She found out where I was staying from that place you and I met. She came out to tell me that my mother's in hospital in London. Had a bad fall. Her name's Mary Goodnight. What's wrong with that and what do you mean coming busting into my room in the middle of the night waving a gun about? And kindly keep your foul tongue to yourself.' Bond was pleased with his bluster and decided to take the next step towards Mary Goodnight's freedom. He dropped his hands to his sides and turned to the girl. 'Put your hands down, Mary. Mr Scaramanga must have thought there were burglars about when he heard that window bang. Now, I'll get some clothes on and take you out to your car. You've got a long drive back to Kingston. Are you sure you wouldn't rather stay here for the rest of the night? I'm sure Mr Scaramanga could find us a spare room.' He turned back to Mr Scaramanga. 'It's all right, Mr Scaramanga, I'll pay for it.'

Mary Goodnight chipped in. She had dropped her hands. She picked up her small bag from the bed where she had thrown it, opened it and began busying herself with her hair in a fussy, feminine way. She chattered, falling in well with Bond's bland piece of very British 'Now-look-here-my-man-manship'. 'No, honestly, darling, I really think I'd better go. I'd be in terrible trouble if I was late at the office and the Prime Minister, Sir Alexander Bustamante, you know he's just had his eightieth birthday, well he's coming to lunch and you know His Excellency always likes me to do the flowers and arrange the place cards and as a matter of fact,' she turned charmingly towards Mr Scaramanga, 'it's quite a day for me. The party was going to make up thirteen so His Excellency has asked me to be the fourteenth. Isn't that marvellous? But heaven knows what I'm going to look like after tonight. The roads really are terrible in parts aren't they, Mr—er—Scramble. But there it is. And I do apologize for causing all this disturbance and keeping you from your beauty sleep.' She went towards him like the Queen Mother opening a bazaar, her hand outstretched. 'Now you run along off back to bed again and my fiancé' (Thank God she hadn't said James! The girl was inspired!) ' 'll see me safely off the premises. Goodbye, Mr, er . . .'

James Bond was proud of her. It was almost pure Joyce Grenfell. But Scaramanga wasn't going to be taken by any double talk, limey or otherwise. She almost had Bond covered from Scaramanga. He moved swiftly aside. He said, 'Hold it, lady. And you, mister, stand where you are.' Mary Goodnight let her hand drop to her side. She looked inquiringly at Scaramanga as if he had just rejected the cucumber sandwiches. Really! These Americans! The Golden Gun didn't go for polite conversation. It held dead steady between the two of them. Scaramanga said to Bond, 'Okay, I'll buy it. Put her through the window again. Then I've got something to say to you.' He waved his gun at the girl. 'Okay, bimbo. Get going. And don't come trespassing on other people's lands again. Right? And you can tell His friggin' Excellency where to shove his place cards. His writ don't run over the Thunderbird. Mine does. Got the photo? Okay. Don't bust your stays getting through the window.'

Mary Goodnight said icily, 'Very good, Mr, er . . . I will deliver your message. I'm sure the High Commissioner will take more careful note than he has done of your presence on the island. And the Jamaican Government also.'

Bond reached out and took her arm. She was on the edge of overplaying her role. He said, 'Come on, Mary. And please tell mother that I'll be through here in a day or two and I'll be telephoning her from Kingston.' He led her to the window and helped, or rather bundled her out. She gave a brief wave and ran off across the lawn. Bond came away from the window with considerable relief. He hadn't expected the ghastly mess to sort itself out so painlessly.

He went and sat down on his bed. He sat on the pillow. He was reassured to feel the hard shape of his gun against his thighs. He looked across at Scaramanga. The man had put his gun back in the shoulder holster. He leant up against the clothes cupboard and ran his finger reflectively along the black line of his moustache. He said, 'High Commissioner's Office. That also houses the local representative of your famous Secret Service. I suppose Mister Hazard, that your real name wouldn't be James Bond? You showed quite a turn of speed with the gun tonight. I seem to have read somewhere that this man Bond fancies himself with the hardware. I also have information to the effect that he's somewhere in the Caribbean and that he's looking for me. Funny coincidence department, eh?'

Bond laughed easily. 'I thought the Secret Service packed up at the end of the war. Anyway, 'fraid I can't change my identity to suit your book. All you've got to do in the morning is ring up Frome and ask for Mr Tony Hugill, the boss up there, and check on my story. And can you explain how this Bond chap could possibly have tracked you down to a brothel in Sav' La Mar? And what does he want from you anyway?'

Scaramanga contemplated him silently for a while. Then he said, 'Guess he may be lookin' for a shootin' lesson. Be glad to oblige him. But you've got something about Number 3½. That's what I figgered when I hired you. But coincidence doesn't come in that size. Mebbe I should have thought again. I said from the first I smelled cops. That girl may be your fiancée or she may not, but that ploy with the shower bath. That's an old hood's trick. Probably a Secret Service one too. Unless, that is, you were screwin' her.' He raised one eyebrow.

'I was. Anything wrong with that? What have you been doing with the Chinese girl? Playing mahjongg?' Bond got to his feet. He stitched impatience and outrage on his face in equal quantities. 'Now look here, Mr Scaramanga. I've had just about enough of this. Just stop leaning on me. You go around waving that damned gun of yours and acting like God Almighty and insinuating a lot of tommyrot about the Secret Service and you expect me to kneel down and lick your boots. Well, my friend, you've come to the wrong address. If you're dissatisfied with the job I'm doing, just hand over the thousand dollars and I'll be on my way. Who in hell d'you think you are anyway?'

Scaramanga smiled his thin, cruel smile. 'You may be getting wise to that sooner than you think, shamus.' He shrugged. 'Okay, okay. But just you remember this, mister. If it turns out you're not who you say you are, I'll blow you to bits. Get me? And I'll start with the little bits and go on to the bigger ones. Just so it lasts a heck of a long time. Right? Now you'd better get some shut-eye. I've got a meeting with Mr Hendriks at ten in the conference room. And I don't want to be disturbed. After that the whole party goes on an excursion on the railroad I was tellin' you about. It'll be your job to see that that gets properly organized. Talk to the manager first thing. Right? Okay, then. Be seeing ya.' Scaramanga walked into the clothes cupboard, brushed Bond's suit aside and disappeared. There came a decisive click from the next room. Bond got to his feet. He said 'Phew!' at the top of his voice and walked off into the bathroom to wash the last two hours away in the shower.

He awoke at 6.30, by arrangement with that curious extra-sensory alarm clock that some people keep in their heads and that always seems to know the exact time. He put on his bathing trunks and went out to the beach and did his long swim again. When at 7.15 he saw Scaramanga come out of the East Wing followed by the boy carrying his towel, he made for the shore. He listened for the twanging thump of the trampoline and then, keeping well out of sight of it, entered the hotel by the main entrance and moved quickly down the corridor to his room. He listened at his window to make sure the man was still exercising, then he took the master key Nick Nicholson had given him and slipped across the corridor to No. 20 and was quickly inside. He left the door on the latch. Yes, there was his target, lying on the dressing-table. He strode across the room, picked up the gun and slipped out the round in the cylinder that would next come up for firing. He put the gun down exactly as he had found it, got back to the door, listened, and then was out and across the corridor and into his own room. He went back to the window and listened. Yes, Scaramanga was still at it. It was an amateurish ploy that Bond had executed, but it might gain him just that fraction of a second that, he felt it in his bones, was going to be life or death for him in the next twenty-four hours. In his mind, he smelled that slight whiff of smoke that indicated that his cover was smouldering at the edges. At any moment 'Mark Hazard of the Transworld Consortium' might go up in flames like some clumsy effigy on Guy Fawkes Night and James Bond would stand there, revealed, with nothing between him and a possible force of six other gunmen but his own quick hand and the Walther PPK. So every shade of odds that he could shift to his side of the board would be worthwhile. Undismayed by the prospect, in

fact rather excited by it, he ordered a large breakfast, consumed it with relish and after pulling the connecting pin out
of the ballcock in his lavatory he went along to the manager's
office.

Felix Leiter was on duty. He gave a thin managerial smile
and said, 'Good morning, Mr Hazard. Can I help you?' Leiter's
eyes were looking beyond Bond, over his right shoulder. Mr
Hendriks materialized at the desk before Bond could answer.

Bond said, 'Good morning.'

Mr Hendriks replied with his little Germanic bow. He said
to Leiter, 'The telephone operator is saying that there is a
long-distance call from my office in Havana. Where is the
most private place to take it, pliss?'

'Not in your bedroom, sir?'

'Is not sufficiently private.'

Bond guessed that he too had bowled out the microphone.

Leiter looked helpful. He came out from behind his desk.
'Just over here, sir. The lobby telephone. This box is soundproof.'

Mr Hendriks looked stonily at him. 'And the machine.
That also is soundproof?'

Leiter looked politely puzzled. 'I'm afraid I don't understand, sir. It is connected directly with the operator.'

'Is no matter. Show me, pliss.' Mr Hendriks followed
Leiter to the far corner of the lobby and was shown into the
booth. He carefully closed the leather-padded door and
picked up the receiver and talked into it. Then he stood
waiting, watching Leiter come back across the marble floor
and speak deferentially to Bond. 'You were saying, sir?'

'It's my lavatory. Something wrong with the ballcock. Is
there anywhere else?'

'I'm so sorry, sir. I'll have the house engineer look at it at once. Yes, certainly. There's the lobby toilet. The decoration isn't completed and it's not officially in use, but it's in perfectly good working order.' He lowered his voice. 'And there's a connecting door with my office. Leave it for ten minutes while I run back the tape of what this bastard's saying. I heard the call was coming through. Don't like the sound of it. May be your worry.' He gave a little bow and waved Bond towards the central table with magazines on it. 'If you'll just take a seat for a few moments, sir, and then I'll take care of you.'

Bond nodded his thanks and turned away. In the booth, Hendriks was talking. His eyes were fixed on Bond with a terrible intensity. Bond felt the skin crawl at the base of his stomach. This was it all right! He sat down and picked up an old *Wall Street Journal*. Surreptitiously he tore a small piece out of the centre of page one. It could have been a tear at the cross-fold. He held the paper up at page two and watched Hendriks through the little hole.

Hendriks watched the back of the paper and talked and listened. He suddenly put down the receiver and came out of the booth. His face gleamed with sweat. He took out a clean white handkerchief and ran it over his face and neck and walked rapidly off down the corridor.

Nick Nicholson, as neat as a pin, came across the lobby and, with a courtly smile and a bow for Bond, took up his place behind the desk. It was 8.30. Five minutes later, Felix Leiter came out from the inner office. He said something to Nicholson and came over to Bond. There was a pale, pinched look round his mouth. He said, 'And now, if you'll follow me, sir.' He led the way across the lobby, unlocked the men's room door, followed Bond in and locked the door behind him. They stood among the carpentry work by the wash-basins. Leiter said tensely, 'I guess you've had it, James. They were talking Russian, but your name and number kept on cropping up. Guess you'd better get out of here just as quickly as that old jalopy of yours'll carry you.'

Bond smiled thinly. 'Forewarned is forearmed, Felix. I knew it already. Hendriks has been told to rub me. Our old friend at KGB headquarters, Semichastny, has got it in for me. I'll tell you why one of these days.' He told Leiter of the Mary Goodnight episode of the early hours. Leiter listened gloomily. Bond concluded, 'So there's no object in getting out now. We shall hear all the dope and probably their plans for me at this meeting at ten. Then they've got this excursion business afterwards. Personally I guess the shooting match'll take place somewhere out in the country where there are no witnesses. Now, if you and Nick could work out something that'd upset the Away Engagement, I'll make myself responsible for the home pitch.'

Leiter looked thoughtful. Some of the cloud lifted from his face. He said, 'I know the plans for this afternoon. Off on this miniature train through the cane fields, picnic, then the boat out of Green Island Harbour, deep-sea fishing and all that. I've reconnoitred the route for it all.' He raised the thumb of his left hand and pinged the end of his steel hook thoughtfully. 'Ye-e-e-s. It's going to mean some quick action and a heap of luck and I'll have to get the hell up to Frome for some supplies from your friend Hugill. Will he hand over some gear on your say-so? Okay, then. Come into my office and write him a note. It's only a half-hour's drive and Nick can hold the front desk for that time. Come on.' He opened a side door and went through into his office. He beckoned Bond to follow and shut the door behind him. At Leiter's dictation, Bond took down the note to the manager of the

WISCO sugar estates and then went out and along to his room. He took a strong nip of straight bourbon and sat on the edge of his bed and looked unseeingly out of the window and across the lawn to the sea's horizon. Like a dozing hound chasing a rabbit in its dreams, or like the audience at an athletics meeting that lifts a leg to help the high-jumper over the bar, every now and then, his right hand twitched involuntarily. In his mind's eye, in a variety of imagined circumstances, it was leaping for his gun.

Time passed and James Bond still sat there, occasionally smoking half-way through a Royal Blend and then absent-mindedly stubbing it out in the bed-table ash-tray. An observer would have made nothing of his thoughts. The pulse in his left temple was beating a little fast. There was some tension, but perhaps only the concentration applied to his thinking, in the slightly pursed lips, but the brooding, blue-grey eyes that saw nothing were relaxed, almost sleepy. It would have been impossible to guess that James Bond was contemplating the possibility of his own death later that day, feeling the soft-nosed bullets tearing into him, seeing his body jerking on the ground, his mouth perhaps screaming. Those were certainly part of his thoughts, but the twitching right hand was evidence that, in much of the whirring film of his thoughts, the enemy's fire was not going unanswered—perhaps had even been anticipated.

James Bond gave a deep relaxed sigh. His eyes came back into focus. He looked at his watch. It said 9.50. He got up, ran both hands down his lean face with a scrubbing motion, and went out and along the corridor to the conference room.

The set-up was the same. Bond's travel literature was on the buffet table where he had left it. He went through into the conference room. It had only been cursorily tidied. Scaramanga had probably said it was not to be entered by the staff. The chairs were roughly in position, but the ash-trays had not been emptied. There were no stains on the carpet and no signs of the carpet having been washed. It had probably been a single shot through the heart. With Scaramanga's soft-nosed bullets, the internal damage would be devastating, but the fragments of the bullet would stay in the body and there would be no bleeding. Bond went round the table, ostentatiously positioning the chairs more accurately. He identified the one where Ruby Rotkopf must have sat, across the table from Scaramanga, because it had a cracked leg. He dutifully examined the windows and looked behind the curtains, doing his job. Scaramanga came into the room followed by Mr Hendriks. He said roughly, 'Okay, Mr Hazard. Lock both doors like yesterday. No one to come in. Right?'

'Yes.' As Bond passed Mr Hendriks he said cheerfully, 'Good morning, Mr Hendriks. Enjoy the party last night?'

Mr Hendriks gave his usual curt bow. He said nothing. His eyes were granite marbles.

Bond went out and locked the doors and took up his position with the brochures and the champagne glass. Immediately, Hendriks began talking, quickly and urgently, fumbling for the English words. 'Mister S. I have bad troubles to report. My Zentrale in Havana spoke with me this morning. They have heard direct from Moscow. This man'— he must have made a gesture towards the door—'this man is the British secret agent, the man Bond. There is no doubt. I am given the exact descriptions. When he goes swimming this morning, I am examining his body through glasses. The wounds on his body are clearly to be seen. The scar down the right side of the face leaves no doubt. And his shooting last night! The ploddy fool is proud of his shooting. I would like to see a member of my organization behave in zees stupid fashions! I would have him shot immediately.' There was a pause. The man's tone altered, became slightly menacing. His target was now Scaramanga. 'But, Mister S. How can this have come about? How can you possibly have let it arrive? My Zentrale is dumbfounded at the mistake. The man might have done much damage but for the watchfulness of my superiors. Please explain, Mister S. I must be making the very full report. How is it that you are meeting this man? How is that you are then carrying him efen into the centre of The Group? The details, pliss, Mister. The full accounting. My superiors will be expressing sharp criticism of the lack of vigilance against the enemy.'

Bond heard the rasp of a match against a box. He could imagine Scaramanga sitting back and going through the smoking routine. The voice, when it came, was decisive, uncowed. 'Mr Hendriks, I appreciate your outfit's concern about this and I congratulate them on their sources of information. But you tell your Central this: I met this man completely by accident, at least I thought so at the time, and there's no use worrying about how it happened. It hasn't been easy to set up this conference and I needed help. I had to get two managers in a hurry from New York to handle the hotel people. They're doing a good job, right? The floor staff and all the rest I had to get from Kingston. But what I really needed was a kind of personal assistant who could be around to make sure that everything went smoothly. Personally, I just couldn't be bothered with all the details. When this guy dropped out of the blue he looked all right to me. So I picked him up. But I'm not stupid. I knew that when this show was over I'd have to get rid of him, just in case he'd learned anything he shouldn't have. Now you say he's a member of the Secret Service. I told you at the beginning of this conference that I eat these people for breakfast when I have a mind to. What you've told me changes just one thing: he'll die today instead of tomorrow. And here's how it's going to happen.' Scaramanga lowered his voice. Now Bond could only hear disjointed words. The sweat ran down from his ear as he pressed it to the base of the champagne glass. 'Our train trip . . . rats in the cane . . . unfortunate accident . . . before I do it . . . one hell of a shock . . . details to myself . . . promise you a big laugh'. Scaramanga must have sat back again. Now his voice was normal. 'So you can rest easy. There'll be nothing left of the guy by this evening. Okay? I could get it over with now by just opening the door. But two blown fuses in two days might stir up gossip around here. And this way there'll be a heap of fun for everyone on the picnic.'

Mr Hendriks' voice was flat and uninterested. He had carried out his orders and action was about to follow, definite action. There could be no complaint of delay in carrying out orders. He said, 'Yes. What you are proposing will be satisfactory. I shall observe the proceedings with much amusement. And now to other business. Plan Orange. My superiors are wishing to know that everything is in order.'

'Yes. Everything's in order at Reynolds Metal, Kaiser Bauxite and Alumina of Jamaica. But your stuff's plenty—what do they call it—volatile. Got to be replaced in the demolition chambers every five years. Hey,' there was a dry chuckle, 'I sure snickered when I saw that the how-do-it labels on the drums were in some of these African languages as well as English. Ready for the big black uprising, huh? You better warn me about The Day. I hold some pretty vulnerable stocks on Wall Street.'

'Then you will lose a lot of money,' said Mr Hendriks flatly. 'I shall not be told the date. I do not mind. I hold no stocks. You would be wise to keep your money in gold or diamonds or rare postage stamps. And now the next matter. It is of interest to my superiors to be able to place their hands on a very great quantity of narcotics. You have a source for the supply of ganja, or marijuana as we call it. You are now receiving your supplies in pound weight. I am asking whether you can stimulate your sources of supply to providing the weed by the hundredweight. It is suggested that you then run shipments to the Pedro Cays. My friends can arrange for collection from there.'

There was a brief silence. Scaramanga would be smoking his thin cheroot. He said, 'Yeah, I think we could swing that. But they've just put some big teeth into these ganja laws. Real rough jail sentences, see? So the goddam price has up and gone through the roof. The going price today is £16 an ounce. A hundredweight of the stuff could cost thousands of pounds. And it's darned bulky in those quantities. My fishing boat could probably only ship one hundredweight at a time. Anyway, where's it for? You'll be lucky to get those quantities ashore. A pound or two is difficult enough.'

'I am not being told the destinations. I assume it is for America. They are the largest consumers. Arrangements have been made to receive this and other consignments initially off the coast of Georgia. I am being told that this area is full of small islands and swamps and is already much favoured by smugglers. The money is of no importance. I have instructions to make an initial outlay of a million dollars, but at keen market prices. You will be receiving your usual ten per cent commission. Is it that you are interested?'

'I'm always interested in a hundred thousand dollars. I'll have to get in touch with my growers. They have their plantations in the Maroon country. That's in the centre of the island. This is going to take time. I can give you a quotation in about two weeks—a hundredweight of the stuff f. o. b. the Pedro Cays. Okay?'

'And a date? The Cays are very flat. This is not stuff to be left lying about, isn't it?'

'Sure. Sure. Now then. Any other business? Okay. Well, I've got something I'd like to bring up. This casino lark. Now, this is the picture. The government are tempted. They think it'll stimulate the tourist industry. But the Heavies—the boys who were kicked out of Havana, the Vegas machine, the Miami jokers, Chicago—the whole works, didn't take the measure of these people before they put the heat on. And they overplayed the slush fund approach—put too much money in the wrong pockets. Guess they should have employed a public relations outfit. Jamaica looks small on the

map, and I guess the Syndicates thought they could hurry
through a neat little operation like the Nassau job. But the
Opposition party got wise, and the Church, and the old
women, and there was talk of the Mafia taking over in Jamaica, the old "Cosa Nostra" and all that crap, and the spiel
flopped. Remember we were offered an "in" couple years
back? That was when they saw it was a bust and wanted to
unload their promotion expenses, couple million bucks or
so, on to The Group. You recall I advised against and gave
my reasons. Okay. So we said no. But things have changed.
Different party in power, bit of a tourist slump last year, and
a certain Minister has been in touch with me. Says the cli-
mate's changed. Independence has come along and they've
got out from behind the skirts of Aunty England. Want to
show that Jamaica's with it. Got oomph and all that. So this
friend of mine says he can get gambling off the pad here. He
told me how and it makes sense. Before, I said stay out. Now
I say come in. But it's going to cost money. Each of us'll have
to chip in with a hundred thousand bucks to give local en-
couragement. Miami'll be the operators and get the fran-
chise. The deal is that they'll put us in for five per cent—but
off the top. Get me? On these figures, and they're not loaded,
our juice should have been earned in eighteen months. After
that it's gravy. Get the photo? But your, er, friends, don't
seem too keen on these, er, capitalist enterprises. How do
you figure it? Will they ante up? I don't want for us to go outside for the green. And, as from yesterday, we're missing a
shareholder. Come to think of it, we've got to think of that
too. Who we goin' to rope in as Number Six? We're short of
a game for now.'

James Bond wiped his ear and the bottom of the glass with
his handkerchief. It was almost unbearable. He had heard his

own death sentence pronounced, the involvement of the KGB with Scaramanga and the Caribbean spelled out, and such minor dividends as sabotage of the bauxite industry, massive drug smuggling into the States and gambling politics thrown in. It was a majestic haul in area Intelligence. He had the ball! Could he live to touch down with it? God, for a drink! He put his ear back to the hot base of the glass.

There was silence. When it came, the voice of Hendriks was cautious, indecisive. He obviously wanted to say 'I pass'—with the corollary, 'until I've talked to my Zentrale, isn't it?'

He said, 'Mister S. Is difficult pizzness, yes? My superiors are not disliking the profitable involvements but, as you will be knowing, they are most liking the pizzness that has the political objective. It was on these conditions that they instructed me to ally myself with your Group. The money, that is not the problem. But how am I to explain the political objective of opening casinos in Jamaica? This I am wondering.'

'It'll almost certainly lead to trouble. The locals'll want to play—they're terrific gamblers here. There'll be incidents. Coloured people'll be turned away from the doors for one reason or another. Then the Opposition party'll get hold of that and raise hell about colour bars and so on. With all the money flying about, the unions'll push wages through the roof. It can all add up to a fine stink. The atmosphere's too damn peaceful around here. This'll be a cheap way of raising plenty of hell. That's what your people want, isn't it? Give the islands the hot foot one after another?'

There was another brief silence. Mr Hendriks obviously didn't like the idea. He said so, but obliquely: 'What you are saying, Mister S, is very interesting. But is it not that these troubles you envisage will endanger our monies? However, I will report your inquiry and inform you at once. It is possible that my superiors will be sympathetic. Who can be telling? Now there is this question of a new Number Six. Are you having anyone in mind?'

'I think we want a good man from South America. We need a guy to oversee our operations in British Guiana. We oughta get smartened up in Venezuela. How come we never got further with that great scheme for blocking the Maracaibo Bar? Like robbing a blind man, given a suitable block ship. Just the threat of it would make the oil companies shell out—that's a joke by the way—and go on shelling by way of protection. Then, if this narcotics spiel is going to be important, we can't do without Mexico. How about Mr Arosio of Mexico City?'

'I am not knowing this gentleman.'

'Rosy? Oh, he's a great guy. Runs the Green Light Transportation System. Drugs and girls into L.A. Never been caught yet. Reliable operator. Got no affiliates. Your people'll know about him. Why not check with them and then we'll put it up to the others? They'll go along with our say-so.'

'Is good. And now, Mister S. Have you anything to report about your own employer? On his recent visit to Moscow, I understand that he expressed satisfaction with your efforts in this area. It is a matter for gratification that there should be such close co-operation between his subversive efforts and our own. Both our chiefs are expecting much in the future from our union with the Mafia. Myself I am doubting. Mr Gengerella is undoubtedly a valuable link, but it is my impression that these people are only being activated by money. What is it that you are thinking?'

'You've said it, Mr Hendriks. In the opinion of my chief, the Mafia's first and only consideration is the Mafia. It has always been so and it always will be so. My Mister C is not expecting great results in the States. Even the Mafia can't buck the anti-Cuban feeling there. But he thinks we can achieve plenty in the Caribbean by giving them odd jobs to do. They can be very effective. It would certainly oil the wheels if your people would use the Mafia as a pipeline for this narcotics business. They'll turn your million-dollar investment into ten. They'll grab the nine out of it of course. But that's not peanuts, and it'll tie them in to you. Think you could arrange that? It'll give Leroy G some good news to report when he gets home. As for Mister C, he seems to be going along all right. Flora was a body-blow but, largely thanks to the Americans leaning on Cuba the way they do, he's kept the country together. If the Americans once let up on their propaganda and needling and so forth, perhaps even make a friendly gesture or two, all the steam'll go out of the little man. I don't often see him. He leaves me alone. Likes to keep his nose clean, I guess. But I get all the co-operation I need from the DSS. Okay? Well let's go see if the folks are ready to move. It's eleven-thirty and the Bloody Bay Belle is due to be on her way at twelve. Guess it's going to be quite a fun day. Pity our Chiefs aren't going to be along to see the limey eye get his chips.'

'Ha!' said Mr Hendriks noncommittally.

James Bond moved away from the door. He heard Mr Scaramanga's pass key in the lock. He looked up and yawned.

Mr Scaramanga and Mr Hendriks looked down at him. Their expressions were vaguely interested and reflective. It was as if he were a bit of steak and they were wondering whether to have it done rare or medium rare.

At twelve o'clock they all assembled in the lobby. Scaramanga had added a broad-brimmed white Stetson to his immaculate tropical attire. He looked like the smartest plantation owner in the South. Mr Hendriks wore his usual stuffy suit, now topped with a grey Homburg. Bond thought that he should have grey suede gloves and an umbrella. The four hoods were wearing calypso shirts outside their slacks. Bond was pleased. If they were carrying guns in their waistbands, the shirts would hinder the draw. Cars were drawn up outside with Scaramanga's Thunderbird in the lead. Scaramanga walked up to the desk. Nick Nicholson was standing washing his hands in invisible soap and looking helpful. 'All set? Everything loaded on the train? Green Harbour been told? Okay, then. Where's that sidekick of yours, that man Travis? Haven't seen him around today.'

Nick Nicholson looked serious. 'He got an abscess in his tooth, sir. Real bad. Had to send him in to Sav' La Mar to have it out. He'll be okay by this afternoon.'

'Too bad. Dock him half a day's pay. No room for sleepers

on this outfit. We're short-handed as it is. Should have had his snappers attended to before he took the job on. 'Kay?'

'Very good, Mr Scaramanga. I'll tell him.'

Mr Scaramanga turned to the waiting group. 'Okay, fellers. Now this is the spiel. We drive a mile down the road to the station. We get aboard this little train. Quite an outfit that. Feller by the name of Lucius Beebe had it copied for the Thunderbird company from the engine and rolling stock on the little old Denver, South Park and Pacific line. Okay. So we steam along this old cane-field line about twenty miles to Green Island Harbour. Plenty birds, bush rats, crocs in the rivers. Mebbe we get a little hunting. Have some fun with the hardware. All you guys got your guns with you? Fine, fine. Champagne lunch at Green Island and the girls and the music'll be there to keep us happy. After lunch we get aboard the *Thunder Girl*, big Chriscraft, and take a cruise along to Lucea, that's a little township down the coast, and see if we can catch our dinner. Those that don't want to fish can play stud. Right? Then back here for drinks. Okay? Everyone satisfied? Any suggestions? Then let's go.'

Bond was told to get in the back of the car. They set off. Once again that offered neck! Crazy not to take him now! But it was open country with no cover and there were four guns riding behind. The odds simply weren't good enough. What was the plan for his removal? During the 'hunting' presumably. James Bond smiled grimly to himself. He was feeling happy. He wouldn't have been able to explain the emotion. It was a feeling of being keyed up, wound taut. It was the moment, after twenty passes, when you got a hand you could bet on—not necessarily win, but bet on. He had been after this man for over six weeks. Today, this morning perhaps, was to come the pay-off he had been ordered to bring about.

It was win or lose. The odds? Foreknowledge was playing for him. He was more heavily forearmed than the enemy knew. But the enemy had the big battalions on their side. There were more of them. And, taking only Scaramanga, perhaps more talent. Weapons? Again leaving out the others, Scaramanga had the advantage. The long-barrelled Colt .45 would be a fraction slower on the draw, but its length of barrel would give it more accuracy than the Walther automatic. Rate of fire? The Walther should have the edge—and the first empty chamber of Scaramanga's gun, if it hadn't been discovered, would be an additional bonus. The steady hand? The cool brain? The sharpness of the lust to kill? How did they weigh up? Probably nothing to choose on the first two. Bond might be a shade trigger-happy—of necessity. That he must watch. He must damp down the fire in his belly. Get ice-cold. In the lust to kill, perhaps he was the strongest. Of course. He was fighting for his life. The other man was just amusing himself—providing sport for his friends, displaying his potency, showing off. That was good! That might be decisive! Bond said to himself that he must increase the other man's unawareness, his casual certitude, his lack of caution. He must be the P. G. Wodehouse Englishman, the limey of the cartoons. He must play easy to take. The adrenalin coursed into James Bond's bloodstream. His pulse rate began to run a fraction high. He felt it on his wrist. He breathed deeply and slowly to bring it down. He found that he was sitting forward, tensed. He sat back and tried to relax. All of his body relaxed except his right hand. This was in the control of someone else. Resting on his right thigh, it still twitched slightly from time to time like the paw of a sleeping dog chasing rabbits. He put it into his coat pocket and watched a turkey buzzard a thousand feet up, circling. He put himself into the mind of the 'John Crow', watching out for a squashed toad or a dead bush rat. The circling buzzard had found its offal. It came lower and lower. Bond wished it 'bon appétit'. The predator in him wished the scavenger a good meal. He smiled at the comparison between them. They were both following a scent. The main difference was that the John Crow was a protected bird. No one would shoot back at it when it made its final dive. Amused by his thoughts, Bond's right hand came out of his pocket and lit a cigarette for him, quietly and obediently. It had stopped going off chasing rabbits on its own.

The station was a brilliant mock-up from the Colorado narrow-gauge era—a low building in faded clapboard ornamented with gingerbread along its eaves. Its name 'Thunderbird Halt' was in old-style ornamental type, heavily seriffed. Advertisements proclaimed 'Chew Roseleaf Fine Cut Warranted Finest Virginia Leaf,' 'Trains Stop for all Meals', 'No Checks Accepted'. The engine, gleaming in black and yellow varnish and polished brass, was a gem. It stood, panting quietly in the sunshine, a wisp of black smoke curling up from the tall stack behind the big brass headlight. The engine's name 'The Belle' was on a proud brass plate on the gleaming black barrel and its number, 'No. 1', on a similar plate below the headlight. There was one carriage, an open affair with padded foam-rubber seats and a daffodil Surrey roof of fringed canvas to keep off the sun, and then the brake van, also in black and yellow, with a resplendent gilt-armed chair behind the conventional wheel of the brake. It was a wonderful toy even down to the old-fashioned whistle which now gave a sharp admonitory blast.

Scaramanga was in ebullient form. 'Hear the train blow, folks! All aboard!' There was an anticlimax. To Bond's dismay he took out his golden pistol, pointed it at the sky and pressed the trigger. He hesitated only momentarily and fired again. The deep boom echoed back from the wall of the station and the station-master, resplendent in old-fashioned uniform, looked nervous. He pocketed the big silver turnip watch he had been holding and stood back obsequiously, the green flag now drooping at his side. Scaramanga checked his gun. He looked thoughtfully at Bond and said, 'All right, my friend. Now then, you get up front with the driver.'

Bond smiled happily. 'Thanks. I've always wanted to do that since I was a child. What fun!'

'You've said it,' said Scaramanga. He turned to the others. 'And you, Mr Hendriks. In the first seat behind the coal-tender, please. Then Sam and Leroy. Then Hal and Louie. I'll be up back in the brake van. Good place to watch out for game. 'Kay?'

Everybody took their seats. The station-master had recovered his nerve and went through his ploy with the watch and the flag. The engine gave a triumphant hoot and, with a series of diminishing puffs, got under way and they bowled off along the three-foot gauge line that disappeared, as straight as an arrow, into a dancing shimmer of silver.

Bond read the speed gauge. It said twenty. For the first time he paid attention to the driver. He was a villainous-looking Rastafari in dirty khaki overalls with a sweat rag round his forehead. A cigarette drooped from between the thin moustache and the straggling beard. He smelled quite horrible. Bond said, 'My name's Mark Hazard. What's yours?'

'Rass, man! Ah doan talk wid buckra.'

The expression 'rass' is Jamaican for 'shove it'. 'Buckra' is a tough colloquialism for 'white man'.

Bond said equably, 'I thought part of your religion was to love thy neighbour.'

The Rasta gave the whistle halyard a long pull. When the shriek had died away, he simply said 'Sheeit', kicked the furnace door open and began shovelling coal.

Bond looked surreptitiously round the cabin. Yes. There it was! The long Jamaican cutlass, this one filed to an inch blade with a deadly point. It was on a rack by the man's hand. Was this the way he was supposed to go? Bond doubted it. Scaramanga would do the deed in a suitably dramatic fashion and one that would give him an alibi. Second executioner would be Hendriks. Bond looked back over the low coal-tender. Hendriks' eyes, bland and indifferent, met his. Bond shouted above the iron clang of the engine, 'Great fun, what?' Hendriks' eyes looked away and back again. Bond stooped so that he could see under the top of the Surrey. All the other four men were sitting motionless, their eyes also fixed on Bond. Bond waved a cheerful hand. There was no response. So they had been told! Bond was a spy in their midst and this was his last ride. In mobese, he was 'going to be hit'. It was an uncomfortable feeling having those ten enemy eyes watching him like ten gun barrels. Bond straightened himself. Now the top half of his body, like the iron 'man' in a pistol range, was above the roof of the Surrey and he was looking straight down the flat yellow surface to where Scaramanga sat on his solitary throne, perhaps twenty feet away, with all his body in full view. He also was looking down the little train at Bond—the last mourner in the funeral cortège behind the cadaver that was James Bond. Bond waved a cheery hand and turned back. He opened his coat and got a moment's reassurance from the cool butt of his gun. He felt in his trouser pocket. Three spare magazines.

Ah, well! He'd take as many of them as he could with him. He flipped down the co-driver's seat and sat on it. No point in offering a target until he had to. The Rasta flicked his cigarette over the side and lit another. The engine was driving herself. He leant against the cabin wall and looked at nothing.

Bond had done his homework on the 1:50,000 Overseas Survey map that Mary had provided and he knew exactly the route the little cane line took. First there would be five miles of the cane fields between whose high green walls they were now travelling. Then came Middle River, followed by the vast expanse of swamplands, now being slowly reclaimed, but still shown on the map as 'The Great Morass'. Then would come Orange River leading into Orange Bay, and then more sugar and mixed forest and agricultural smallholdings until they came to the little hamlet of Green Island at the head of the excellent anchorage of Green Island Harbour.

A hundred yards ahead, a turkey buzzard rose from beside the line and, after a few heavy flaps, caught the inshore breeze and soared up and away. There came the boom of Scaramanga's gun. A feather drifted down from the great right-hand wing of the big bird. The turkey buzzard swerved and soared higher. A second shot rang out. The bird gave a jerk and began to tumble untidily down out of the sky. It jerked again as a third bullet hit it before it crashed into the cane. There was applause from under the yellow Surrey. Bond leant out and called to Scaramanga, 'That'll cost you five pounds unless you've squared the Rasta. That's the fine for killing a John Crow.'

A shot whistled past Bond's head. Scaramanga laughed. 'Sorry. Thought I saw a rat.' And then, 'Come on, Mr Hazard.

Let's see some gun play from you. There's some cattle graz-
ing by the line up there. See if you can hit a cow at ten
paces.'

The hoods guffawed. Bond put his head out again. Scaramanga's gun was on his lap. Out of the corner of his eye he
saw that Mr Hendriks, perhaps ten feet behind him, had his
right hand in his coat pocket. Bond called, 'I never shoot
game that I don't eat. If you'll eat the whole cow, I'll shoot it
for you.'

The gun flashed and boomed as Bond jerked his head
under cover of the coal-tender. Scaramanga laughed harshly.
'Watch your lip, limey, or you'll end up without it.' The
hoods haw-hawed.

Beside Bond, the Rasta gave a curse. He pulled hard on the
whistle lanyard. Bond looked down the line. Far ahead,
across the rails, something pink showed. Still whistling, the
driver pulled on a lever. Steam belched from the train's exhaust and the engine began to slow. Two shots rang out and
the bullets clanged against the iron roof over his head.
Scaramanga shouted angrily, 'Keep steam up, damn you to
hell!'

The Rasta quickly pushed up the lever and the speed of
the train gathered back to 20 mph. He shrugged. He glanced
at Bond. He licked his lips wetly. 'Dere's white trash across
de line. Guess mebbe it's some frien' of de boss.'

Bond strained his eyes. Yes! It was a naked pink body with
golden blonde hair! A girl's body!

Scaramanga's voice boomed against the wind. 'Folks. Jes'
a little surprise for you all. Something from the good old
Western movies. There's a girl on the line ahead. Tied across
it. Take a look. And you know what? It's the girl friend of a

certain man we've been hearing of called James Bond. Would you believe it? An' her name's Goodnight, Mary Goodnight. It sure is goodnight for her. If only that fellow Bond was aboard now, I guess we'd be hearing him holler for mercy.'

James Bond leaped for the accelerator lever and tore it down-wards. The engine lost a head of steam but there was only a hundred yards to go and now the only thing that could save the girl was the brakes under Scaramanga's control in the brake van. The Rasta already had his cutlass in his hand. The flames from the furnace glinted on the blade. He stood back like a cornered animal, his eyes red with ganja and fear of the gun in Bond's hand. Nothing could save the girl now! Bond, knowing that Scaramanga would expect him from the right side of the tender, leaped to the left. Hendriks had his gun out. Before it could swivel, Bond put a bullet between the man's cold eyes. The head jerked back. For an instant, steel-capped back teeth showed in the gaping mouth. Then the grey Homburg fell off and the dead head slumped. The golden gun boomed twice. A bullet whanged round the cabin. The Rasta screamed and fell to the ground, clutching at his throat. His hand was still clenched round the whistle lanyard and the little train kept up its mournful howl of warning. Fifty yards to go! The golden hair hung forlornly forward, obscuring the face. The ropes on the wrists and an-

kles showed clearly. The breasts offered themselves to the
screaming engine. Bond ground his teeth and shut his mind
to the dreadful impact that would come any minute now. He
leaped to the left again and got off three shots. He thought
two of them had hit, but then something slammed a great
blow into the muscle of his left shoulder and he spun across
the cab and crashed to the iron floor, his face over the edge
of the footplate. And it was from there, only inches away,
that he saw the front wheels scrunch through the body on
the line, saw the blonde head severed from the body, saw the
china-blue eyes give him a last blank stare, saw the fragments of the showroom dummy disintegrate with a sharp
crackling of plastic and the pink splinters shower down the
embankment.

James Bond choked back the sickness that rose from his
stomach into the back of his throat. He staggered to his feet,
keeping low. He reached up for the accelerator lever and
pushed it upwards. A pitched battle with the train at a
standstill would put the odds even more against him. He
hardly felt the pain in his shoulder. He edged round the
right-hand side of the tender. Four guns boomed. He flung
his head back under cover. Now the hoods were shooting,
but wildly because of the interference of the Surrey top. But
Bond had had time to see one glorious sight. In the brake
van, Scaramanga had slid from his throne and was down on
his knees, his head moving to and fro like a wounded animal. Where in hell had Bond hit him? And now what? How
was he going to deal with the four hoods, just as badly ob-
scured from him as he was from them?

Then a voice from the back of the train, it could only be
from the brake van, Felix Leiter's voice, called out above the
shriek of the engine's whistle, 'Okay, you four guys. Toss

your guns over the side. Now! Quick!' There came the crack
of a shot. 'I said quick! There's Mr Gengerella gone to meet
his maker. Okay, then. And now hands behind your heads.
That's better. Right. Okay, James. The battle's over. Are you
okay? If so, show yourself. There's still the final curtain and
we've got to move quick.'

Bond rose carefully. He could hardly believe it! Leiter
must have been riding on the buffers behind the brake van.
He wouldn't have been able to show himself earlier for fear
of Bond's gunfire. Yes! There he was! His fair hair tousled by
the wind, a long-barrelled pistol using his upraised steel
hook as a rest, standing astride the now supine body of
Scaramanga beside the brake wheel. Bond's shoulder had
begun to hurt like hell. He shouted, with the anger of
tremendous relief, 'God damn you, Leiter. Why in hell didn't
you show up before? I might have got hurt.'

Leiter laughed. 'That'll be the day! Now listen, shamus.
Get ready to jump. The longer you wait, the farther you've
got to walk home. I'm going to stay with these guys for a
while and hand them over to the law in Green Harbour.' He
shook his head to show this was a lie. 'Now get goin'. It's The
Morass. The landing'll be soft. Stinks a bit, but we'll give you
an eau-de-Cologne spray when you get home. Right?'

The train ran over a small culvert and the song of the
wheels changed to a deep boom. Bond looked ahead. In the
distance was the spidery iron work of the Orange River
bridge. The still shrieking train was losing steam. The gauge
said 19 mph. Bond looked down at the dead Rasta. In death,
his face was as horrible as it had been in life. The bad teeth,
sharpened from eating sugar cane from childhood, were
bared in a frozen snarl. Bond took a quick glance under the
Surrey. Hendriks' slumped body lolled with the movement

of the train. The sweat of the day still shone on the doughy
cheeks. Even as a corpse he didn't ask for sympathy. In the
seat behind him, Leiter's bullet had torn through the back of
Gengerella's head and removed most of his face. Next to him,
and behind him, the three gangsters gazed up at James Bond
with whipped eyes. They hadn't expected all this. This was
to have been a holiday. The calypso shirts said so. Mr Scaramanga, the undefeated, the undefeatable, had said so. Until
minutes before, his golden gun had backed up his word.
Now, suddenly, everything was different. As the Arabs say
when a great sheikh has gone, has removed his protection,
'Now there is no more shade!' They were covered with guns
from the front and rear. The train stretched out its iron stride
towards nowhere they had ever heard of before. The whistle
moaned. The sun beat down. The dreadful stink of The Great
Morass assailed their nostrils. This was abroad. This was bad
news, really bad. The Tour Director had left them to fend for
themselves. Two of them had been killed. Even their guns
were gone. The tough faces, as white moons, gazed in sup-
plication up at Bond. Louie Paradise's voice was cracked and
dry with terror. 'A million bucks, Mister, if you get us out of
this. Swear on my mother. A million.'

The faces of Sam Binion and Hal Garfinkel lit up. Here
was hope! 'And a million.'

'And another! On my baby son's head!'

The voice of Felix Leiter bellowed angrily. There was a
note of panic in it. 'Jump, damn you James! Jump!

James Bond stood up in the cabin, not listening to the
voices supplicating from under the yellow Surrey. These
men had wanted to watch him being murdered. They had
been prepared to murder him themselves. How many dead
men had each one of them got on his tally-sheet? Bond got

down on the step of the cabin, chose his moment and threw himself clear of the clinker track and into the soft embraces of a stinking mangrove pool.

His explosion into the mud released the stench of hell. Great bubbles of marsh gas wobbled up to the surface and burst glutinously. A bird screeched and clattered off through the foliage. James Bond waded out on to the edge of the embankment. Now his shoulder was really hurting. He knelt down and was as sick as a cat.

When he raised his head it was to see Leiter hurl himself off the brake van, now a good two hundred yards away. He seemed to land clumsily. He didn't get up. And now, within yards of the long iron bridge over the sluggish river, another figure leaped from the train into a clump of mangrove. It was a tall, chocolate-clad figure. There was no doubt about it! It was Scaramanga! Bond cursed feebly. Why in hell hadn't Leiter put a finishing bullet through the man's head? Now there was unfinished business. The cards had only been reshuffled. The end game had still to be played!

The screaming progress of the driverless train changed to a roar as the track took to the trestles of the long bridge. Bond watched it vaguely, wondering when it would run out of steam. What would the three gangsters do now? Take to the hills? Get the train under control and go on to Green Harbour and try and take the *Thunder Girl* across to Cuba? Immediately the answer came! Half-way across the bridge, the engine suddenly reared up like a bucking stallion. At the same time there came a crash of thunder and a vast sheet of flame and the bridge buckled downwards in the centre like a bent leg. Chunks of torn iron sprayed upwards and sideways and there was a splintering crash as the main stanchions gave and slowly bowed down towards the water. Through the jagged gap, the beautiful Belle, a smashed toy, folded upon itself and, with a giant splintering of iron and woodwork and a volcano of spray and steam, thundered into the river.

A deafening silence fell. Somewhere behind Bond, a wakened tree frog tinkled uncertainly. Four white egrets flew down and over the wreck, their necks outstretched inquisitively. In the distance, black dots materialized high up in the sky and circled lazily closer. The sixth sense of the turkey buzzards had told them that the distant explosion was disaster—something that might yield a meal. The sun hammered down on the silver rails and, a few yards away from where Bond lay, a group of yellow butterflies danced in the shimmer. Bond got slowly to his feet and, parting the butterflies, began walking slowly but purposefully up the line towards the bridge. First Felix Leiter and then after the big one that had got away.

Leiter lay in the stinking mud. His left leg was at a hideous angle. Bond went down to him, his finger to his lips. He knelt beside him and said softly, 'Nothing much I can do for now, pal. I'll give you a bullet to bite on and get you into some shade. There'll be people coming before long. Got to get on after that bastard. He's somewhere up there by the bridge. What made you think he was dead?'

Leiter groaned, more in anger with himself than from the pain. 'There was blood all over the place.' The voice was a halting whisper between clenched teeth. 'His shirt was soaked in it. Eyes closed. Thought if he wasn't cold he'd go with the others on the bridge.' He smiled faintly. 'How did you dig the River Kwai stunt? Go off all right?'

Bond raised a thumb. 'Fourth of July. The crocs'll be sitting down to table right now. But that damned dummy! Gave me a nasty turn. Did you put her there?'

'Sure. Sorry, boy. Mr S. told me to. Made an excuse to spike the bridge this morning. No idea your girl friend was a blonde or that you'd fall for the spiel.'

'Bloody silly of me, I suppose. Thought he'd got hold of her last night. Anyway, come on. Here's your bullet. Bite the lead. The story-books say it helps. This is going to hurt, but I must haul you under cover and out of the sun.' Bond got his hands under Leiter's armpits and, as gently as he could, dragged him to a dry patch under a big mangrove bush above swamp level. The sweat of pain poured down Leiter's face. Bond propped him up against the roots. Leiter gave a groan and his head fell back. Bond looked thoughtfully down at him. A faint was probably the best thing that could have happened. He took Leiter's gun out of his waistband and put it beside his left, and only, hand. Bond still might get into much trouble. If he did, Scaramanga would come after Felix.

Bond crept off along the line of mangroves towards the bridge. For the time being he would have to keep more or less in the open. He prayed that, nearer the river, the swamp would yield to drier land so that he could work down towards the sea and then cut back towards the river and hope to pick up the man's tracks.

It was 1.30 and the sun was high. James Bond was hungry and very thirsty and his shoulder wound throbbed with his pulse. The wound was beginning to give him a fever. One dreams all day as well as all night, and now, as he stalked his prey, he found, quizzically, that much of his mind was taken up with visualizing the champagne buffet waiting for them all, the living and the dead, at Green Harbour. For the moment, he indulged himself. The buffet would be laid out under the trees, as he saw it, adjoining the terminal station, which would probably be on the same lines as Thunderbird

Halt. There would be long trestle tables, spotless tablecloths, rows of glasses and plates and cutlery and great dishes of cold lobster salad, cold meat cuts, and mounds of fruit— pineapple and such—to make the décor look Jamaican and exotic. There might be a hot dish, he thought. Something like roast stuffed suckling-pig with rice and peas—too hot for the day, decided Bond, but a feast for most of Green Harbour when the rich 'tourists' had departed. And there would be drink! Champagne in frosted silver coolers, rum punches, Tom Collinses, whisky sours, and, of course, great beakers of iced water that would only have been poured when the train whistled its approach to the gay little station. Bond could see it all. Every detail of it under the shade of the great ficus trees. The white-gloved, uniformed coloured waiters enticing him to take more and more; beyond, the dancing waters of the harbour, in the background the hypnotic throb of the calypso band, the soft, enticing eyes of the girls. And, ruling, ordering all, the tall, fine figure of the gracious host, a thin cigar between his teeth, the wide white Stetson tilted low over his brow, offering Bond just one more goblet of iced champagne.

James Bond stumbled over a mangrove root, threw out his right hand for support from the bush, missed, tripped again and fell heavily. He lay for a moment, measuring the noise he must have made. It wouldn't have been much. The inshore wind from the sea was feathering the swamp. A hundred yards away the river added its undertone of sluggish turbulence. There were cricket and bird noises. Bond got to his knees and then to his feet. What in hell had he been thinking of? Come on, you bloody fool! There's work to be done! He shook his head to clear it. Gracious host! God damn it! He was on his way to kill the gracious host! Goblets of iced champagne? That'd be the day! He shook his head angrily. He took several very deep slow breaths. He knew the symptoms. This was nothing worse than acute nervous exhaustion with—he gave himself that amount of grace—a small fever added. All he had to do was to keep his mind and his eyes in focus. For God's sake no more day-dreaming! With a new sharpened resolve he kicked the mirages out of his mind and looked to his geography.

There were perhaps a hundred yards to go to the bridge. On Bond's left, the mangroves were sparser and the black mud was dry and cracked. But there were still soft patches. Bond put up the collar of his coat to hide the white shirt. He covered another twenty yards beside the rail and then struck off left into the mangroves. He found that if he kept close to the roots of the mangroves the going wasn't too bad. At least there were no dry twigs or leaves to crack and rustle. He tried to keep as nearly as possible parallel with the river, but thick patches of bushes made him make small detours and he had to estimate his direction by the dryness of the mud and the slight rise of the land towards the river bank. His ears were pricked like an animal's for the smallest sound. His eyes strained into the greenery ahead. Now the mud was pitted with the burrows of land crabs and there were occasional remnants of their shells, victims of big birds or mongoose. For the first time, mosquitoes and sand-flies began to attack him. He could not slap them off but only dab at them softly with his handkerchief that was soon soaked with the blood they had sucked from him and wringing with the white man's sweat that attracted them.

Bond estimated that he had penetrated two hundred yards into the swamp when he heard the single, controlled cough.

The cough sounded about twenty yards away, towards the river. Bond dropped to one knee, his senses questing like the antennae of an insect. He waited five minutes. When the cough was not repeated, he crept forward on hands and knees, his gun gripped between his teeth.

In a small clearing of dried, cracked black mud, he saw the man. He stopped in his tracks, trying to calm his breathing.

Scaramanga was lying stretched out, his back supported by a clump of sprawling mangrove roots. His hat and his high stock had gone and the whole of the right-hand side of his suit was black with blood upon which insects crawled and feasted. But the eyes in the controlled face were still very much alive. They swept the clearing at regular intervals, questing. Scaramanga's hands rested on the roots beside him. There was no sign of a gun.

Scaramanga's face suddenly pointed, like a retriever's, and the roving scrutiny held steady. Bond could not see what had caught his attention, but then a patch of the dappled shadow at the edge of the clearing moved and a large snake, beautifully diamonded in dark and pale brown, zigzagged purposefully across the black mud towards the man.

Bond watched, fascinated. He guessed it was a boa of the *Epicrates* family, attracted by the smell of blood. It was perhaps five feet long and quite harmless to man. Bond wondered if Scaramanga would know this. He was immediately put out of his doubt. Scaramanga's expression had not changed, but his right hand crept softly down his trouser leg, gently pulled up the cuff and removed a thin, stiletto-style knife from the side of his short Texan boot. Then he waited, the knife held ready across his stomach, not clenched in his fist, but pointed in the flick-knife fashion. The snake paused for a moment a few yards from the man and raised its head high to give him a final inspection. The forked tongue licked out inquisitively, again and again, then, still with its head held above the ground, it moved slowly forward.

Not a muscle moved in Scaramanga's face. Only the eyes were dead steady, watchful slits. The snake came into the shadow of his trouser leg and moved slowly up towards the glistening shirt. Suddenly the tongue of steel that lay across Scaramanga's stomach came to life and leaped. It transfixed the head of the snake exactly in the centre of the brain and pierced through it, pinning it to the ground and holding it there while the powerful body thrashed wildly, seeking a grip on the mangrove roots, on Scaramanga's arm. But immediately, when it had a grip, its convulsions released its coils which flailed off in another direction.

The death struggles diminished and finally ceased altogether. The snake lay motionless. Scaramanga was careful. He ran his hand down the full length of the snake. Only the tip of the tail lashed briefly. Scaramanga extracted the knife from the head of the snake, cut off its head with a single hard stroke and threw it, after reflection, accurately towards a crab hole. He waited, watching, to see if a crab would come out and take it. None did. The thud of the arrival of the snake's head would have kept any crab underground for many minutes, however enticing the scent of what had made the thud.

James Bond, kneeling in the bush, watched all this, every nuance of it, with the most careful attention. Each one of Scaramanga's actions, every fleeting expression on his face, had been an index of the man's awareness, of his aliveness. The whole episode of the snake was as revealing as a temperature chart or a lie-detector. In Bond's judgement, Mr Scaramanga, for all his blood-letting and internal injuries, was still very much alive. He was still a most formidable and dangerous man.

Scaramanga, his task satisfactorily completed, minutely shifted his position, and, once again, foot by foot, made his penetrating examination of the surrounding bush.

As Scaramanga's gaze swept by him without a flicker, Bond blessed the darkness of his suit—a black patch of shadow among so many others. In the sharp blacks and whites from the midday sun, Bond was well camouflaged.

Satisfied, Scaramanga picked up the limp body of the snake, laid it across his stomach and carefully slit it down its underside as far as the anal vent. Then he scoured it and carefully etched the skin away from the red-veined flesh with the precise flicks and cuts of a surgeon. Every scrap of unwanted reptile he threw towards crab holes and, with each throw, a flicker of annoyance crossed the granite face that no one would come and pick up the crumbs from the rich man's table. When the meal was ready, he once again scanned the bush and then, very carefully, coughed and spat into his hand. He examined the results and flung his hand sideways. On the black ground, the sputum made a bright pink scrawl. The cough didn't seem to hurt him or cause him much effort. Bond guessed that his bullet had hit Scaramanga in the right chest and had missed a lung by a fraction. There was haemorrhage and Scaramanga was a hospital case, but the blood-soaked shirt was not telling the whole truth.

Satisfied with his inspection of his surroundings, Scaramanga bit into the body of the snake and was at once, like a dog with its meal, absorbed by his hunger and thirst for the blood and juices of the snake.

Bond had the impression that, if he now came forward from his hiding-place, Scaramanga, like a dog, would bare his teeth in a furious snarl. He got quietly up from his knees, took out his gun and, his eyes watching Scaramanga's hands, strolled out into the centre of the little clearing.

Bond was mistaken. Scaramanga did not snarl. He barely looked up from the cut-off length of snake in his two hands and, his mouth full of meat, said, 'You've been a long while coming. Care to share my meal?'

'No thanks. I prefer my snake grilled with hot butter sauce. Just keep on eating. I like to see both hands occupied.'

Scaramanga sneered. He gestured at his blood-stained shirt. 'Frightened of a dying man? You limeys come pretty soft.'

'The dying man handled that snake quite efficiently. Got any more weapons on you?' As Scaramanga moved to undo his coat, 'Steady! No quick movements. Just show your belt, armpits, pat the thighs inside and out. I'd do it myself only I don't want what the snake got. And while you're about it, just toss the knife into the trees. Toss. No throwing, if you don't mind. My trigger-finger's been getting a bit edgy today. Seems to want to go about its business on its own. Wouldn't like it to take over. Yet, that is.'

Scaramanga, with a flick of his wrist, tossed the knife into the air. The sliver of steel spun like a wheel in the sunshine. Bond had to step aside. The knife pierced the mud where Bond had been standing and stood upright. Scaramanga gave a harsh laugh. The laugh turned into a cough. The gaunt face contorted painfully. Too painfully? Scaramanga spat red, but not all that red. There could be only slight haemorrhage. Perhaps a broken rib or two. Scaramanga could be out of hospital in a couple of weeks. Scaramanga put down his piece of snake and did exactly as Bond had told him, all the while watching Bond's face with his usual cold, arrogant stare. He finished and picked up the piece of snake and began gnawing it. He looked up. 'Satisfied?'

'Sufficiently.' Bond squatted down on his heels. He held his gun loosely, aiming somewhere halfway between the two of them. 'Now then, let's talk. 'Fraid you haven't got too much time, Scaramanga. This is the end of the road. You've killed too many of my friends. I have the licence to kill you and I am going to kill you. But I'll make it quick. Not like Margesson. Remember him? You put a shot through both of his knees and both of his elbows. Then you made him crawl and kiss your boots. You were foolish enough to boast about it to your friends in Cuba. It got back to us. As a matter of interest, how many men have you killed in your life?'

'With you, it'll make the round fifty.' Scaramanga had gnawed the last segment of backbone clean. He tossed it towards Bond. 'Eat that, scum, and get on with your business. You won't get any secrets out of me, if that's your spiel. An' don't forget. I've been shot at by experts an' I'm still alive.

Mebbe not precisely kicking but I've never heard of a limey who'd shoot a defenceless man who's badly wounded. They ain't got the guts. We'll just sit here, chewing the fat, until the rescue team comes. Then I'll be glad to go for trial. What'll they get me for eh?'

'Well, just for a start, there's that nice Mr Rotkopf with one of your famous silver bullets in his head in the river back of the hotel.'

'That'll match with the nice Mr Hendriks with one of your bullets somewhere behind his face. Mebbe we'll serve a bit of time together. That'd be nice, wouldn't it? They say the jail at Spanish Town has all the comforts. How about it, limey? That's where you'll be found with a shiv in your back in the sack-sewing department.

An' by the same token, how d'you know about Rotkopf?'

'Your bug was bugged. Seems you're a bit accident-prone these days, Scaramanga. You hired the wrong security men. Both your managers were from the CIA. The tape'll be on the way to Washington by now. That's got the murder of Ross on it too. See what I mean? You've got it coming from every which way.'

'Tape isn't evidence in an American court. But I see what you mean, shamus. Mistakes seem to have got made. So okay,' Scaramanga made an expansive gesture of the right hand. 'Take a million bucks and call it quits?'

'I was offered three million on the train.'

'I'll double that.'

'No. Sorry.' Bond got to his feet. The left hand behind his back was clenched with the horror of what he was about to do. He forced himself to think of what the broken body of Margesson must have looked like, of the others that this man had killed, of the ones he would kill afresh if Bond weakened. This man was probably the most efficient one-man death dealer in the world. James Bond had him. He had been instructed to take him. He must take him—lying down wounded, or in any other position. Bond assumed casualness, tried to make himself the enemy's cold equal. 'Any messages for anyone, Scaramanga? Any instructions? Anyone you want looking after? I'll take care of it if it's personal. I'll keep it to myself.'

Scaramanga laughed his harsh laugh, but carefully. This time the laugh didn't turn into the red cough. 'Quite the little English gentleman! Just like I spelled it out. S'pose you wouldn't like to hand me your gun and leave me to myself for five minutes like in the books? Well, you're right, boyo! I'd crawl after you and blast the back of your head off.' The eyes still bored into Bond's with the arrogant superiority, the cold superman quality that had made him the greatest pro gunman in the world—no drinks, no drugs—the impersonal trigger man who killed for money and, by the way he sometimes did it, for the kicks.

Bond examined him carefully. How could Scaramanga fail to break when he was going to die in minutes? Was there some last trick the man was going to spring? Some hidden weapon? But the man just lay there, apparently relaxed, propped up against the mangrove roots, his chest heaving rhythmically, the granite of his face not crumbling even minutely in defeat. On his forehead, there was not as much sweat as there was on Bond's. Scaramanga lay in dappled black shadow. For ten minutes, James Bond had stood in the middle of the clearing in blazing sunshine. Suddenly he felt the vitality oozing out through his feet into the black mud. And his resolve was going with it. He said, and he heard his voice ring out harshly, 'All right, Scaramanga, this it it.' He lifted his gun and held it in the two-handed grip of the target man. 'I'm going to make it as quick as I can.'

Scaramanga held up a hand. For the first time his face showed emotion. 'Okay, feller.' The voice, amazingly, supplicated. 'I'm a Catholic, see? Jes' let me say my last prayer. Okay? Won't take long, then you can blaze away. Every man's got to die some time. You're a fine guy as guys go. It's the luck of the game. If my bullet had been an inch, mebbe two inches, to the right, it'd be you that's dead in place of me. Right? Can I say my prayer, Mister?'

James Bond lowered his gun. He would give the man a few minutes. He knew he couldn't give him more. Pain and heat and hunger and thirst. It wouldn't be long before he lay down himself, right there on the hard cracked mud, just to rest. If someone wanted to kill him, they could. He said, and the words came out slowly, tiredly, 'Go ahead, Scaramanga. One minute only.'

'Thanks, pal.' Scaramanga's hand went up to his face and covered his eyes. There came a drone of Latin which went on and on. Bond stood there in the sunshine, his gun lowered, watching Scaramanga, but at the same time not watching him, the edge of his focus dulled by the pain and the heat and the hypnotic litany that came from behind the shuttered face and the horror of what Bond was going to have to do—in one minute, perhaps two.

The fingers of Scaramanga's right hand crawled imperceptibly sideways across his face, inch by inch, centimetre by centimetre. They got to his ear and stopped. The drone of the Latin prayer never altered its slow, lulling tempo.

And then the hand leaped behind the head and the tiny golden Derringer roared and James Bond spun round as if he had taken a right to the jaw and crashed to the ground.

At once Scaramanga was on his feet and moving forward like a swift cat. He snatched up the discarded knife and held it forward like a tongue of silver flame.

But James Bond twisted like a dying animal on the ground and the iron in his hand cracked viciously again and again— five times, and then fell out of his hand on to the black earth as his gun-hand went to the right side of his belly and stayed there, clutching at the terrible pain.

The big man stood for a moment and looked up at the deep blue sky. His fingers opened in a spasm and let go the knife. His pierced heart stuttered and limped and stopped. He crashed flat back and lay, his arms flung wide, as if someone had thrown him away.

After a while, the land crabs came out of their holes and began nosing at the scraps of the snake. The bigger offal could wait until the night.

The extremely smart policeman from the wrecking squad on the railway came down the river bank at the normal, dignified gait of a Jamaican constable on his beat. No Jamaican policeman ever breaks into a run. He has been taught that this lacks authority. Felix Leiter, now put under with morphine by the doctor, had said that a good man was after a bad man in the swamp and that there might be shooting. Felix Leiter wasn't more explicit than that, but, when he said he was from the FBI—a legitimate euphemism—in Washington, the policeman tried to get some of the wrecking squad to come with him and, when he failed, sauntered cautiously off on his own, his baton swinging with assumed jauntiness.

The boom of the guns and the explosion of screeching marsh birds gave him an approximate fix. He had been born not far away, at Negril, and, as a boy, he had often used his gins and his slingshot in these marshes. They held no fears for him. When he came to the approximate point on the river bank, he turned left into the mangrove and, conscious that his black-and-blue uniform was desperately conspicuous, stalked cautiously from clump to clump into the morass. He was protected by nothing but his nightstick and the knowledge that to kill a policeman was a capital offence without the option. He only hoped that the good man and the bad man knew this too.

With all the birds gone, there was dead silence. The constable noticed that the tracks of bush rats and other small animals were running past him on a course that converged with his target area. Then he heard the rattling scuttle of the crabs and, in a moment, from behind a thick mangrove clump, he saw the glint of Scaramanga's shirt. He watched and listened. There was no movement and no sound. He strolled, with dignity, into the middle of the clearing, looked at the two bodies and the guns and took out his nickel police whistle and blew three long blasts. Then he sat down in the shade of a bush, took out his report pad, licked his pencil and began writing in a laborious hand.

A week later, James Bond regained consciousness. He was in a green-shaded room. He was under water. The slowly revolving fan in the ceiling was the screw of a ship that was about to run him down. He swam for his life. But it was no good. He was tied down, anchored to the bottom of the sea. He screamed at the top of his lungs. To the nurse at the end of the bed it was the whisper of a moan. At once she was beside him. She put a cool hand on his forehead. While she took his pulse, James Bond looked up at her with unfocused eyes. So this was what a mermaid looked like! He muttered 'You're pretty,' and gratefully swam back down into her arms.

The nurse wrote ninety-five on his sheet and telephoned down to the ward sister. She looked in the dim mirror and tidied her hair in preparation for the RMO in charge of this apparently Very Important Patient.

The Resident Medical Officer, a young Jamaican graduate from Edinburgh, arrived with the matron, a kindly dragon on loan from King Edward VII's. He heard the nurse's report. He went over to the bed and gently lifted Bond's eyelids. He slipped a thermometer under Bond's armpit and held Bond's pulse in one hand and a pocket chronometer in the other and there was silence in the little room. Outside, the traffic tore up and down a Kingston road.

The doctor released Bond's pulse and slipped the chronometer back into the trouser pocket under the white smock. He wrote figures on the chart. The nurse held the door open and the three people went out into the corridor. The doctor talked to the matron. The nurse was allowed to listen. 'He's going to be all right. Temperature well down. Pulse a little fast but that may have been the result of his waking. Reduce the antibiotics. I'll talk to the floor sister about that later. Keep on with the intravenous feeding. Dr Macdonald will be up later to attend to the dressings. He'll be waking again. If he asks for something to drink, give him fruit juice. He should be on soft foods soon. Miracle really. Missed the abdominal viscera. Didn't even shave a kidney. Muscle only. That bullet was dipped in enough poison to kill a horse. Thank God that man at Sav' La Mar recognized the symptoms of snake venom and gave him those massive anti-snake bite injections. Remind me to write to him, matron. He saved the man's life. Now then, no visitors of course, for at least another week. You can tell the police and the High Commissioner's Office that he's on the mend. I don't know who he is, but apparently London keep on worrying us about him. Something to do with the Ministry of Defence. From now on, put them and all other inquiries through to the High Commissioner's Office. They seem to think they're in charge of him.' He paused. 'By the way, how's his friend getting on in Number Twelve? The one the American Ambassador and Washington have been on about. He's not on my list, but he keeps on asking to see this Mr Bond.'

'Compound fracture of the tibia,' said the matron. 'No complications.' She smiled. 'Except that he's a bit fresh with the nurses. He should be walking with a stick in ten days. He's already seen the police. I suppose it's all to do with that story in the *Gleaner* about those American tourists being killed when the bridge collapsed near Green Island Harbour. But the Commissioner's handling it all personally. The story in the *Gleaner*'s very vague.'

The doctor smiled. 'Nobody tells me anything. Just as well. I haven't got the time to listen to them. Well, thank you, matron. I must get along. Multiple crash at Halfway Tree. The ambulances'll be here any minute.' He hurried away. The matron went about her business. The nurse, excited by all this high-level talk, went softly back into the green-shaded room, tidied the sheet over the naked right shoulder of her patient where the doctor had pulled it down, and went back to her chair at the end of the bed and her copy of *Ebony*.

Ten days later, the little room was crowded. James Bond, propped up among extra pillows, was amused by the galaxy of officialdom that had been assembled. On his left was the Commissioner of Police, resplendent in his black uniform with silver insignia. On his right was a Judge of the Supreme Court in full regalia accompanied by a deferential clerk. A massive figure, to whom Felix Leiter, on crutches, was fairly respectful, had been introduced as 'Colonel Bannister' from Washington. Head of Station C, a quiet civil servant called

Alec Hill, who had been flown out from London, stood near
the door and kept his appraising eyes unwaveringly on
Bond. Mary Goodnight, who was to take notes of the proceedings but also, on the matron's strict instructions, watch
for any sign of fatigue in James Bond and have absolute authority to close the meeting if he showed strain, sat demurely
beside the bed with a shorthand pad on her knees. But James
Bond felt no strain. He was delighted to see all these people
and know that at last he was back in the great world again.
The only matters that worried him were that he had not been
allowed to see Felix Leiter before the meeting to agree their
stories and that he had been rather curtly advised by the
High Commissioner's Office that legal representation would
not be necessary.

The Police Commissioner cleared his throat. He said,
'Commander Bond, our meeting here today is largely a for-
mality, but it is held on the Prime Minister's instructions and
with your doctor's approval. There are many rumours running around the island and abroad and Sir Alexander Bustamante is most anxious to have them dispelled for the sake of
justice and of the island's good name. So this meeting is in
the nature of a judicial inquiry having Prime Ministerial status. We very much hope that, if the conclusions of the meeting are satisfactory, there need be no more legal proceedings
whatever. You understand?'

'Yes,' said Bond, who didn't.

'Now,' the Commissioner spoke weightily. 'The facts as as-
certained are as follows. Recently there took place at the
Thunderbird Hotel in the Parish of Westmoreland a meeting
of what can only be described as foreign gangsters of outstanding notoriety, including representatives of the Soviet
Secret Service, the Mafia, and the Cuban Secret Police. The

objects of this meeting were, inter alia, sabotage of Jamaican installations in the cane industry, stimulation of illicit ganja-growing in the island and purchase of the crop for export, the bribery of a high Jamaican official with the object of installing gangster-run gambling in the island and sundry other malfeasances deleterious to law and order in Jamaica and to her international standing. Am I correct, Commander?'

'Yes,' said Bond, this time with a clear conscience.

'Now.' The Commissioner spoke with even greater emphasis. 'The intentions of this subversive group became known to the Criminal Investigation Department of the Jamaican Police and the facts of the proposed assembly were placed before the Prime Minister in person by myself. Naturally the greatest secrecy was observed. A decision then had to be reached as to how this meeting was to be kept under surveillance and penetrated so that its intentions might be learned. Since friendly nations, including Britain and the United States, were involved, secret conversations took place with the representatives of the Ministry of Defence in Britain and of the Central Intelligence Agency in the United States. As a result, export personnel in the shape of yourself, Mr Nicholson and Mr Leiter were generously made available, at no cost to the Jamaican Government, to assist in unveiling these secret machinations against Jamaica held on Jamaican soil.' The Commissioner paused and looked round the room to see if he had stated the position correctly. Bond had noticed that Felix Leiter nodded his head vigorously with the others, but, in his case, in Bond's direction.

Bond smiled. He had at last got the message. He also nodded his agreement.

'Accordingly,' continued the Commissioner, 'and working throughout under the closest liaison and direction of the Ja-

maican CID, Messrs Bond, Nicholson and Leiter carried out
their duties in exemplary fashion. The true intentions of the
gangsters were unveiled, but alas, in the process, the identity
of at least one of the Jamaica-controlled agents was discovered and a battle royal took place during the course of which
the following enemy agents—here there will be a list—were
killed, thanks to the superior gunfire of Commander Bond
and Mr Leiter, and the following—another list—by the destruction by Mr Leiter's ingenious use of explosive of the Orange River Bridge on the Lucea–Green Island Harbour
railway, now converted for tourist use. Unfortunately, two of
the Jamaica-controlled agents received severe wounds from
which they are now recovering in the Memorial Hospital. It
remains to mention the names of Constable Percival Samp-
son of the Negril Constabulary who was first on the scene of
the final battlefield, and Dr Lister Smith of Savannah La Mar
who rendered vital first aid to Commander Bond and Mr
Leiter. On the instructions of the Prime Minister, Sir Alexander Bustamante, a judicial inquiry was held this day at the
bedside of Commander Bond and in the presence of Mr Felix
Leiter to confirm the above facts. These, in the presence of
Justice Morris Cargill of the Supreme Court, are now and
hereby confirmed.'

The Commissioner was obviously delighted with his rendering of all this rigmarole. He beamed at Bond. 'It only remains', he handed Bond a sealed packet, a similar one to
Felix Leiter and one to Colonel Bannister, 'to confer on Commander Bond of Great Britain, Mr Felix Leiter of the United
States and, in absentia, Mr Nicholas Nicholson of the United
States, the immediate award of the Jamaican Police Medal
for gallant and meritorious services to the Independent State
of Jamaica.'

There was muted applause. Mary Goodnight went on clapping after the others had stopped. She suddenly realized the fact, blushed furiously and stopped.

James Bond and Felix Leiter made stammered acknowledgements. Justice Cargill rose to his feet and, in solemn tones, asked Bond and Leiter in turn, 'Is this a true and correct account of what occurred between the given dates?'

'Yes, indeed,' said Bond.

'I'll say it is, Your Honour,' said Felix Leiter fervently.

The Judge bowed. All except Bond rose and bowed. Bond just bowed. 'In that case, I declare this inquiry closed.' The bewigged figure turned to Miss Goodnight. 'If you will be kind enough to obtain all the signatures, duly witnessed, and send them round to my chambers? Thank you so much.' He paused and smiled. 'And the carbon, if you don't mind?'

'Certainly, my lord.' Mary Goodnight glanced at Bond. 'And now, if you will forgive me, I think the patient needs a rest. Matron was most insistent . . .'

Goodbyes were said. Bond called Leiter back. Mary Goodnight smelled private secrets. She admonished, 'Now, only a minute!' and went out and closed the door.

Leiter leant over the end of the bed. He wore his most quizzical smile. He said, 'Well, I'll be goddamned, James. That was the neatest wrap-up job I've ever lied my head off at. Everything clean as a whistle and we've even collected a piece of lettuce.'

Talking starts with the stomach muscles. Bond's wounds were beginning to ache. He smiled, not showing the pain. Leiter was due to leave that afternoon. Bond didn't want to say goodbye to him. Bond treasured his men friends and Felix Leiter was a great slice of his past. He said, 'Scaramanga was quite a guy. He should have been taken alive.

Maybe Tiffy really did put the hex on him with Mother Edna. They don't come like that often.'

Leiter was unsympathetic. 'That's the way you limeys talk about Rommel and Dönitz and Guderian. Let alone Napoleon. Once you've beaten them, you make heroes out of them. Don't make sense to me. In my book, an enemy's an enemy. Care to have Scaramanga back? Now, in this room, with his famous golden gun on you—the long one or the short one? Standing where I am? One bets you a thousand you wouldn't. Don't be a jerk, James. You did a good job. Pest control. It's got to be done by someone. Going back to it when you're off the orange juice?' Felix Leiter jeered at him. 'Of course you are, lamebrain. It's what you were put into the world for. Pest control, like I said. All you got to figure is how to control it better. The pests'll always be there. God made dogs. He also made their fleas. Don't let it worry your tiny mind. Right?' Leiter had seen the sweat on James Bond's forehead. He limped towards the door and opened it. He raised his hand briefly. The two men had never shaken hands in their lives. Leiter looked into the corridor. He said, 'Okay, Miss Goodnight. Tell matron to take him off the danger list. And tell him to keep away from me for a week or two. Every time I see him a piece of me gets broken off. I don't fancy myself as The Vanishing Man.' Again he raised his only hand in Bond's direction and limped out.

Bond shouted, 'Wait, you bastard!' But, by the time Leiter had limped back into the room, Bond, no effort left in him to fire off the volley of four-letter words that were his only answer to his friend, had lapsed into unconsciousness.

Mary Goodnight shooed the remorseful Leiter out of the room and ran off down the corridor to the floor sister.

A week later, James Bond was sitting up in a chair, a towel round his waist, reading Allen Dulles on *The Craft of Intelligence* and cursing his fate. The hospital had worked miracles on him, the nurses were sweet, particularly the one called 'The Mermaid', but he wanted to be off and away. He glanced at his watch. Four o'clock. Visiting time. Mary Goodnight would soon be there and he would be able to let off his pent-up steam on her. Unjust perhaps, but he had already tongue-lashed everyone in range in the hospital and, if she got into the field of fire, that was just too bad!

Mary Goodnight came through the door. Despite the Jamaican heat, she was looking fresh as a rose. Damn her! She was carrying what looked like a typewriter. Bond recognized it as the Triple-X decyphering machine. Now what?

Bond grunted surly answers to her inquiries after his health. He said, 'What in hell's that for?'

'It's an "Eyes Only". Personal from M,' she said excitedly. 'About thirty groups.'

'Thirty groups! Doesn't the old bastard know I've only got

one arm that's working? Come on, Mary. You get cracking. If it sounds really hot, I'll take over.'

Mary Goodnight looked shocked. 'Eyes Only' was a top secret prefix. But Bond's jaw was jutting out dangerously. Today was not a day for argument. She sat on the edge of the bed, opened the machine and took a cable form out of her bag. She laid her shorthand book beside the machine, scratched the back of her head with her pencil to help work out the setting for the day—a complicated sum involving the date and the hour of dispatch of the cable—adjusted the setting on the central cylinder and began cranking the handle. After each completed word had appeared in the little oblong window at the base of the machine, she recorded it in her book.

James Bond watched her expression. She was pleased. After a few minutes she read out: 'M PERSONAL FOR 007 EYES ONLY STOP YOUR REPORT AND DITTO FROM TOP FRIENDS [a euphemism for the CIA] RECEIVED STOP YOU HAVE DONE WELL AND EXECUTED AYE DIFFICULT AND HAZARDOUS OPERATION TO MY ENTIRE REPEAT ENTIRE SATISFACTION STOP TRUST YOUR HEALTH UNIMPAIRED [Bond gave an angry snort] STOP WHEN WILL YOU BE REPORTING FOR FURTHER DUTY QUERY.'

Mary Goodnight smiled delightedly. 'I've never seen him be so complimentary! Have you, James? That repeat of ENTIRE! It's tremendous!' She looked hopefully for a lifting of the black clouds from Bond's face.

In fact Bond was secretly delighted, but he certainly wasn't going to show it to Mary Goodnight. Today she was one of the wardresses confining him, tying him down. He said grudgingly, 'Not bad for the old man. But all he wants is to get me back to that bloody desk. Anyway, it's a lot of jazz so far. What comes next?' He turned the pages of his book, pretending as the little machine whirred and clicked not to be interested.

'Oh, James!' Mary Goodnight exploded with excitement. 'Wait! I'm almost finished. It's tremendous!'

'I know,' commented Bond sourly. 'Free luncheon vouchers every second Friday. Key to M's personal lavatory. New suit to replace the one that's somehow got full of holes.' But he kept his eyes fixed on the flitting fingers, infected by Mary Goodnight's excitement. What in hell was she getting so steamed up about? And all on his behalf! He examined her with approval. Perched there, immaculate in her white tussore shirt and tight beige skirt, one neat foot curled round the other in concentration, the golden face under the shortish fair hair incandescent with pleasure, she was, thought Bond, a girl to have around always. As secretary? As what? Mary Goodnight turned, her eyes shining, and the question went, as it had gone for weeks, without an answer.

'Now, just listen to this, James.' She shook the notebook at him. 'And for heaven's sake stop looking so curmudgeonly.'

Bond smiled at the word. 'All right, Mary. Go ahead. Empty the Christmas stocking on the floor. Hope it's not going to bust any stitches.' He put his book down on his lap.

Mary Goodnight's face became portentous. She said seriously, 'Just listen to this!' She read very carefully: 'IN VIEW OF THE OUTSTANDING NATURE OF THE SERVICES REFERRED TO ABOVE AND THEIR ASSISTANCE TO THE ALLIED CAUSE COMMA WHICH IS PERHAPS MORE SIGNIFICANT THAN YOU IMAGINE COMMA THE PRIME MINISTER PROPOSES TO RECOMMEND TO HER MAJESTY QUEEN ELIZABETH THE IMMEDIATE GRANT OF A KNIGHTHOOD STOP THIS TO TAKE THE FORM OF THE ADDITION OF A KATIE AS PREFIX TO YOUR CHARLIE MICHAEL GEORGE. [James Bond uttered a defensive, embarrassed laugh. 'Good old cypherines. They wouldn't think of just putting KCMG—much too easy! Go ahead, Mary. This is good!'] IT IS COMMON PRACTICE TO INQUIRE OF PROPOSED RECIPIENT WHETHER HE ACCEPTS THIS HIGH HONOUR BEFORE HER MAJESTY PUTS HER SEAL UPON IT STOP WRITTEN LETTER SHOULD FOLLOW YOUR CABLED CONFIRMATION OF ACCEPTANCE PARAGRAPH THIS AWARD NATURALLY HAS MY SUPPORT AND ENTIRE APPROVAL AND EYE SEND YOU MY PERSONAL CONGRATULATIONS ENDIT MAILEDFIST.'

James Bond again hid himself behind the throw-away line. 'Why in hell does he always have to sign himself "Mailedfist" for "M"? There's a perfectly good English word "Em". It's a measure used by printers. But of course it's not dashing enough for the Chief. He's a romantic at heart like all the silly bastards who get mixed up with the Service'.

Mary Goodnight lowered her eyelashes. She knew that Bond's reflex concealed his pleasure—a pleasure he wouldn't for the life of him have displayed. Who wouldn't be pleased, proud? She put on a businesslike expression. 'Well, would you like me to draft something for you to send? I can be back with it at six and I know they'll let me in. I can check up on the right sort of formula with the High Commissioner's staff. I know it begins with "I present my humble duty to Her Majesty". I've had to help with the Jamaica honours at New Year and her birthday. Everyone seems to want to know the form.'

James Bond wiped his forehead with his handkerchief. Of course he was pleased! But above all pleased with M's commendation. The rest, he knew, was not in his stars. He had never been a public figure and he did not wish to become one. He had no prejudice against letters after one's name, or before it. But there was one thing above all he treasured. His privacy. His anonymity. To become a public person, a person, in the snobbish world of England, of any country, who would be called upon to open things, lay foundation stones, make after-dinner speeches, brought the sweat to his armpits. 'James Bond'! No middle name. No hyphen. A quiet, dull, anonymous name. Certainly he was a Commander in the Special Branch of the RNVR, but he rarely used the rank. His CMG likewise. He wore it perhaps once a year, together with his two rows of 'lettuce', because there was a dinner for the 'Old Boys'—the fraternity of ex-Secret Service men that went under the name of 'The Twin Snakes Club'— a grisly reunion held in the banqueting hall at Blades that gave enormous pleasure to a lot of people who had been brave and resourceful in their day but now had old men's and old women's diseases and talked about dusty triumphs and tragedies which, since they would never be recorded in the history books, must be told again that night, over the Cockburn '12, when 'The Queen' had been drunk, to some next-door neighbour such as James Bond who was only interested in what was going to happen tomorrow. That was when he wore his 'lettuce' and the CMG below his black tie—to give pleasure and reassurance to the 'Old Children' at their annual party. For the rest of the year, until May polished them up for the occasion, the medals gathered dust in some secret repository where May kept them.

So now James Bond said to Mary Goodnight, avoiding her eyes, 'Mary, this is an order. Take down what follows and send it tonight. Right? Begins, quote MAILEDFIST EYES ONLY [Bond interjected, 'I might have said PROMONEYPENNY. When did M last touch a cypher machine?'] YOUR [Put in the number, Mary] ACKNOWLEDGED AND GREATLY APPRECIATED STOP AM INFORMED BY HOSPITAL AUTHORITIES THAT EYE SHALL BE RETURNED LONDONWARDS DUTIABLE IN ONE MONTH STOP REFERRING YOUR REFERENCE TO AYE HIGH HONOUR EYE BEG YOU PRESENT MY HUMBLE

DUTY TO HER MAJESTY AND REQUEST THAT EYE MAY BE PERMITTED COMMA IN ALL HUMILITY COMMA TO DECLINE THE SIGNAL FAVOUR HER MAJESTY IS GRACIOUS ENOUGH TO PROPOSE TO CONFER UPON HER HUMBLE AND OBEDIENT SERVANT BRACKET TO MAILEDFIST PLEASE PUT THIS IN THE APPROPRIATE WORDS TO THE PRIME MINIS- TER STOP MY PRINCIPAL REASON IS THAT EYE DONT WANT TO PAY MORE AT HOTELS AND RESTAURANTS BRACKET.'

Mary Goodnight broke in, horrified. 'James. The rest is your business, but you really can't say that last bit.'

Bond nodded. 'I was only trying it on you, Mary. All right, let's start again at the last stop. Right. EYE AM A SCOTTISH PEAS- ANT AND WILL ALWAYS FEEL AT HOME BEING A SCOTTISH PEASANT AND EYE KNOW COMMA SIR COMMA THAT YOU WILL UNDERSTAND MY PREFERENCE AND THAT EYE CAN COUNT ON YOUR INDULGENCE BRACKET LETTER CONFIRMING FOLLOWS IMMEDIATELY ENDIT OHOH- SEVEN.'

Mary Goodnight closed her book with a snap. She shook her head. The golden hair danced angrily. 'Well really, James! Are you sure you don't want to sleep on it? I knew you were in a bad mood today. You may have changed your mind by tomorrow. Don't you want to go to Buckingham Palace and see the Queen and the Duke of Edinburgh and kneel and have your shoulder touched with a sword and the Queen to say "Arise, Sir Knight" or whatever it is she does say?'

Bond smiled. 'I'd like all those things. The romantic streak of the SIS—and of the Scot, for the matter of that. I just re- fuse to call myself Sir James Bond. I'd laugh at myself every time I looked in the mirror to shave. It's just not my line, Mary. The thought makes me positively shudder. I know M'll understand. He thinks much the same way about these things as I do. Trouble was, he had to more or less inherit his

K with the job. Anyway, there it is and I shan't change my mind so you can buzz that off and I'll write M a letter of confirmation this evening. Any other business?'

'Well there is one thing, James.' Mary Goodnight looked down her pretty nose. 'Matron says you can leave at the end of the week, but that there's got to be another three weeks' convalescence. Had you got any plans where to go? You have to be in reach of the hospital.'

'No ideas. What do you suggest?'

'Well, er, I've got this little villa up by Mona dam, James.' Her voice hurried. 'It's got quite a nice spare room looking out over Kingston harbour. And it's cool up there. And if you don't mind sharing a bathroom.' She blushed. 'I'm afraid there's no chaperone, but you know, in Jamaica, people don't mind that sort of thing.'

'What sort of thing?' said Bond, teasing her.

'Don't be silly, James. You know, unmarried couples sharing the same house and so on.'

'Oh, that sort of thing! Sounds pretty dashing to me. By the way, is your bedroom decorated in pink, with white jalousies, and do you sleep under a mosquito net?'

She looked surprised. 'Yes. How did you know?' When he didn't answer, she hurried on. 'And James, it's not far from the Liguanea Club and you can go there and play bridge, and golf when you get better. There'll be plenty of people for you to talk to. And then of course I can cook and sew buttons on for you and so on.'

Of all the doom-fraught graffiti a woman can write on the wall, those are the most insidious, the most deadly.

James Bond, in the full possession of his senses, with his eyes wide open, his feet flat on the linoleum floor, stuck his head blithely between the mink-lined jaws of the trap. He said, and meant it, 'Goodnight. You're an angel.'

At the same time, he knew, deep down, that love from Mary Goodnight, or from any other woman, was not enough for him. It would be like taking 'a room with a view'. For James Bond, the same view would always pall.

FOR THE BEST IN PAPERBACKS, LOOK FOR THE

In every corner of the world, on every subject under the sun, Penguin represents quality and variety—the very best in publishing today.

For complete information about books available from Penguin—including Penguin Classics, Penguin Compass, and Puffins—and how to order them, write to us at the appropriate address below. Please note that for copyright reasons the selection of books varies from country to country.

In the United States: Please write to *Penguin Group (USA), P.O. Box 12289 Dept. B, Newark, New Jersey 07101-5289* or call *1-800-788-6262*.

In the United Kingdom: Please write to *Dept. EP, Penguin Books Ltd, Bath Road, Harmondsworth, West Drayton, Middlesex UB7 0DA.*

In Canada: Please write to *Penguin Books Canada Ltd, 90 Eglinton Avenue East, Suite 700, Toronto, Ontario M4P 2Y3.*

In Australia: Please write to *Penguin Books Australia Ltd, P.O. Box 257, Ringwood, Victoria 3134.*

In New Zealand: Please write to *Penguin Books (NZ) Ltd, Private Bag 102902, North Shore Mail Centre, Auckland 10.*

In India: Please write to *Penguin Books India Pvt Ltd, 11 Panchsheel Shopping Centre, Panchsheel Park, New Delhi 110 017.*

In the Netherlands: Please write to *Penguin Books Netherlands bv, Postbus 3507, NL-1001 AH Amsterdam.*

In Germany: Please write to *Penguin Books Deutschland GmbH, Metzlerstrasse 26, 60594 Frankfurt am Main.*

In Spain: Please write to *Penguin Books S. A., Bravo Murillo 19, 1° B, 28015 Madrid.*

In Italy: Please write to *Penguin Italia s.r.l., Via Benedetto Croce 2, 20094 Corsico, Milano.*

In France: Please write to *Penguin France, Le Carré Wilson, 62 rue Benjamin Baillaud, 31500 Toulouse.*

In Japan: Please write to *Penguin Books Japan Ltd, Kaneko Building, 2-3-25 Koraku, Bunkyo-Ku, Tokyo 112.*

In South Africa: Please write to *Penguin Books South Africa (Pty) Ltd, Private Bag X14, Parkview, 2122 Johannesburg.*